First and Last

Hilaire Belloc

First and Last

The present edition is a reproduction of previous publication of this classic work. Minor typographical errors may have been corrected without note; however, for an authentic reading experience the spelling, punctuation, and capitalization have been retained from the original text.

ISBN: 978-1-63637-014-9

CONTENTS

On Weighing Anchor

Personally I should call it "Getting It up," but I have always seen it in print called "weighing anchor"--and if it is in print one must bow to it. It does weigh.

There are many ways of doing it. The best, like all good things, has gone for ever, and this best way was for a thing called a capstan to have sticking out from it, movable, and fitted into its upper rim, other things called capstan--bars. These, men would push singing a song, while on the top of the capstan sat a man playing the fiddle, or the flute, or some other instrument of music. You and I have seen it in pictures. Our sons will say that they wish they had seen it in pictures. Our sons' sons will say it is all a lie and was never in anything but the pictures, and they will explain it by some myth or other.

Another way is to take two turns of a rope round a donkey-engine, paying in and coiling while the engine clanks. And another way on smaller boats is a sort of jack arrangement by which you give little jerks to a ratchet and wheel, and at last It looses Its hold. Sometimes (in this last way) It will not loose Its hold at all.

Then there is a way of which I proudly boast that it is the only way I know, which is to go forward and haul at the line until It comes--or does not come. If It does not come, you will not be so cowardly or so mean as to miss your tide for such a trifle. You will cut the line and tie a float on and pray Heaven that into whatever place you run, that place will have moorings ready and free.

When a man weighs anchor in a little ship or a large one he does a jolly thing! He cuts himself off and he starts for freedom and for the chance of things. He pulls the jib a-weather, he leans to her slowly pulling round, he sees the wind getting into the mainsail, and he feels that she feels the helm. He has her on a slant of the wind, and he makes out between the harbour piers. I am supposing, for the sake of good luck, that it is not blowing bang down the harbour mouth, nor, for the matter of that, bang out of it. I am supposing, for the sake of good luck to this venture, that in weighing anchor you have the wind so that you can sail with it full and by, or freer still, right past the walls until you are well into the tide outside. You may tell me that you are so rich and your boat is so big that there have been times when you have anchored in the very open, and that all this does not apply to you. Why, then, your thoughts do not apply to me nor to the little boat I have in mind.

In the weighing of anchor and the taking of adventure and of the sea there is an exact parallel to anything that any man can do in the beginning of any human thing, from his momentous setting out upon his life in early manhood to the least decision of his present passing day. It is a very proper emblem of a beginning. It may lead him to that kind of muddle and set-back which attaches only to beginnings, or it may get him fairly into the weather, and yet he may find, a little way outside, that he has to run for it, or to beat back to harbour. Or, more generously, it may lead him to a long and steady cruise in which he shall find profit and make distant rivers and continue to increase his log by one good landfall after another. But the whole point of weighing anchor is that he has chosen his weather and his tide, and that he is setting out. The thing is done.

You will very commonly observe that, in land affairs, if good fortune follows a venture it is due to the marvellous excellence of its conductor, but if ill fortune, then to evil chance alone. Now, it is not so with the sea.

The sea drives truth into a man like salt. A coward cannot long pretend to be brave at sea, nor a fool to be wise, nor a prig to be a good companion, and any venture connected with the sea is full of venture and can pretend to be nothing more. Nevertheless there is a certain pride in keeping a course through different weathers, in making the best of a tide, in using cats' paws in a dull race, and, generally, in knowing how to handle the thing you steer and to judge the water and the wind. Just because men have to tell the truth once they get into tide water, what little is due to themselves in their success thereon they are proud of and acknowledge.

If your sailing venture goes well, sailing reader, take a just pride in it; there will be the less need for me to write, some few years hence, upon the art of picking up moorings, though I confess I would rather have written on that so far as the fun of writing was concerned. For picking up moorings is a far more tricky and amusing business than Getting It up. It differs with every conceivable circumstance of wind, and tide, and harbour, and rig, and freeboard, and light; and then there are so many stories to tell about it! As--how once a poor man picked up a rich man's moorings at Cowes and was visited by an aluminium boat, all splendid in the morning sun. Or again--how a stranger who had made Orford Haven (that very difficult place) on the very top of an equinoctial springtide, picked up a racing mark-buoy, taking it to be moorings, and dragged it with him all the way to Aldborough, and that right before the town of Orford, so making himself hateful to the Orford people.

But I digress....

The Reveillon

There was in the regiment with which I served a man called Frocot, famous with his comrades because he had seen The Dead, for this experience, though common among the Scotch, is rare among the French, a sister nation. This man Frocot could neither write nor read, and was also the strongest man I ever knew. He was quite short and exceedingly broad, and he could break a penny with his hands, but this gift of strength, though young men value it so much, was thought little of compared with his perception of unseen things, for though the men, who were peasants, professed to laugh at it, and him, in their hearts they profoundly believed. It had been made clear to us that he could see and hear The Dead one night in January during a snowstorm, when he came in and woke me in barrack-room because he had heard the Loose Spur. Our spurs were not buckled on like the officers'; they were fixed into the heel of the boot, and if a nail loosened upon either side the spur dragged with an unmistakable noise. There was a sergeant who (for some reason) had one so loosened on the last night he had ever gone the rounds before his death, for in the morning as he came off guard he killed himself, and the story went about among the drivers that sometimes on stable guard in the thick of the night, when you watched all alone by the lantern (with your three comrades asleep in the straw of an empty stall), your blood would stop and your skin tauten at the sound of a loose spur dragging on the far side of the stable, in the dark. But though many had heard the story, and though some had pretended to find proof for it, I never knew a man to feel and know it except this man Frocot on that night. I remember him at the foot of my bed with his lantern waking me from the rooted sleep of bodily fatigue, standing there in his dark blue driver's coat and staring with terrible eyes. He had undoubtedly heard and seen, but whether of himself from within, imagining, or, as I rather believe, from without and influenced, it is impossible to say. He was rough and poor, and he came from the Forest of Ardennes.

The reason I remember him and write of him at this season is not, however, this particular and dreadful visitation of his, but a folly or a vision that befell him at this time of the year, now seventeen years ago; for he had Christmas leave and was on his way from garrison to his native place, and he was walking the last miles of the wood. It was the night before Christmas. It was clear, and there was no wind, but the sky was overcast with level clouds and the evening was very dark. He started unfed since the first meal of

3

the day; it was dark three hours before he was up into the high wood. He met no one during all these miles, and his body and his mind were lonely; he hoped to press on and be at his father's door before two in the morning or perhaps at one. The night was so still that he heard no noise in the high wood, not even the rustling of a leaf or a twig crackling, and no animal ran in the undergrowth. The moss of the ride was silent under his heavy tread, but now and then the steel of his side-arm clicked against a metal button of the great cloak he wore. This sharp sound made him so conscious of himself that he seemed to fill that forest with his own presence and to be all that was, there or elsewhere. He was in a mood of unreal and not holy things. The mood, remaining, changed its aspect, and now he was so far from alone that all the trunks around him and the glimmers of sky between bare boughs held each a spirit of its own, and with the powerful imagination of the unlearned he could have spoken and held communion with the trees; but it would have an evil communion, for he felt this mood of his take on a further phase as he went deeper and deeper still into these forests. He felt about him uneasily the sense of doom. He was in that exaltation of fancy or dream when faint appeals are half heard far off, but not by our human ears, and when whatever attempts to pierce the armour of our mortality appeals to us by wailing and by despairing sighs. It seemed to him that most unhappy things passed near him in the air, and that the wood about him was full of sobbing. Then, again, he felt his own mind within him begin to be occupied by doubtful troubles worse than these terrors, an anxious straining for ill news, for bitter and dreadful news, mixed with a confused certitude that such news had come indeed, disturbed and haunted him; and all the while about him in that stillness the rushing of unhappy spirits went like a secret storm. He was clouded with the mingled emotions of apprehension and of fatal mourning; he attempted to remember the expectations that had failed him, friends untrue, and the names of parents dead; but he was now the victim of this strange night and unable (whether from hunger or fatigue, or from that unique power of his to discern things beyond the world) to remember his life or his definite aims at all, or even his own name. He was mixed with the whole universe about him, and was suffering some loss so grievous that very soon the gait of his march and his whole being were informed by a large and final despair.

It was in this great and universal mood (granted to him as a seer, though he was a common man) that he saw down the ride, but somewhat to one side of it in the heart of the high wood, a great light shining from a barn or shed that stood there in the undergrowth, and to this light, though his way naturally led him to it, he felt also impelled by an influence as strong as or stronger than the despair that had filled his soul and all the woods around. He went on therefore quickly, straining with his eyes, and when he came into the light that shone out from this he saw a more brilliant light within, and men of his own kind adoring; but the vision was confused, like light on light or like vapours moving over bright metals in a cauldron, and as he gazed his mind became still and the dread left him altogether. He said it was like shutting a gentleman's great oaken door against a driving storm.

This is the story he told me weeks after as we rode together in the battery, for he hid it in his heart till the spring. As I say, I believed him.

He was an unlearned man and a strong; he never worshipped. He was of that plain stuff and clay on which has worked since all recorded time the power of the Spirit.

He said that when he left (as he did rapidly leave) that light, peace also left him, but that the haunting terror did not return. He found the clearing and his father's hut; fatigue and the common world indeed returned, but with them a permanent memory of things experienced.

Every word I have written of him is true.

On Cheeses

If antiquity be the test of nobility, as many affirm and none deny (saving, indeed, that family which takes for its motto "Sola Virtus Nobilitas," which may mean that virtue is the only nobility, but which may also mean, mark you, that nobility is the only virtue--and anyhow denies that nobility is tested by the lapse of time), if, I say, antiquity be the only test of nobility, then cheese is a very noble thing.

But wait a moment: there was a digression in that first paragraph which to the purist might seem of a complicated kind.

Were I writing algebra (I wish I were) I could have analysed my thoughts by the use of square brackets, round brackets, twiddly brackets, and the rest, all properly set out in order so that a Common Fool could follow them.

But no such luck! I may not write of algebra here; for there is a rule current in all newspapers that no man may write upon any matter save upon those in which he is more learned than all his human fellows that drag themselves so slowly daily forward to the grave.

So I had to put the thing in the very common form of a digression, and very nearly to forget that great subject of cheese which I had put at the very head and title of this.

Which reminds me: had I followed the rule set down by a London journalist the other day (and of the proprietor of his paper I will say nothing--though I might have put down the remark to his proprietor) I would have hesitated to write that first paragraph. I would have hesitated, did I say? Griffins' tails! Nay--Hippogriffs and other things of the night! I would not have dared to write it at all! For this journalist made a law and promulgated it, and the law was this: that no man should write that English which could not be understood if all the punctuation were left out. Punctuation, I take it, includes brackets, which the Lord of Printers knows are a very modern part of punctuation indeed.

Now let the horripilised reader look up again at the first paragraph (it will do him no harm), and think how it would look all written out in fair uncials like the beautiful Gospels of St. Chad, which anyone may see for nothing in the cathedral of Lichfield, an English town famous for eight or nine different things: as Garrick, Doctor Johnson, and its two opposite inns. Come, read that first paragraph over now and see what you could make of it if it were written out in uncials--that is, not only without punctuation, but without any division between the words. Wow! As the philosopher said when he was asked to give a plain answer "Yes" or "No."

And now to cheese. I have had quite enough of digressions and of follies. They are the happy youth of an article. They are the springtime of it. They are its riot. I am approaching the middle age of this article. Let us be solid upon the matter of cheese.

I have premised its antiquity, which is of two sorts, as is that of a nobleman. First, the antiquity of its lineage; secondly, the antiquity of its self. For we all know that when we meet a nobleman we revere his nobility very much if he be himself old, and that this quality of age in him seems to marry itself in some mysterious way with the antiquity of his line.

The lineage of cheese is demonstrably beyond all record. What did the faun in the beginning of time when a god surprised him or a mortal had the misfortune to come across him in the woods? It is well known that the faun offered either of them cheese. So he knew how to make it.

There are certain bestial men, hangers-on of the Germans, who would contend that this would prove cheese to be acquired by the Aryan race (or what not) from the Dolichocephalics (or what not), and there are certain horrors who descend to imitate these barbarians--though themselves born in these glorious islands, which are so steep upon their western side. But I will not detain you upon these lest I should fall head foremost into another digression and forget that my article, already in its middle age, is now approaching grey hairs.

At any rate, cheese is very old. It is beyond written language. Whether it is older than butter has been exhaustively discussed by several learned men, to whom I do not send you because the road towards them leads elsewhere. It is the universal opinion of all most accustomed to weigh evidence (and in these I very properly include not only such political hacks as are already upon the bench but sweepingly every single lawyer in Parliament, since any one of them may tomorrow be a judge) that milk is older than cheese, and that man had the use of milk before he cunningly devised the trick of squeezing it in a press and by sacrificing something of its sweetness endowed it with a sort of immortality.

The story of all this has perished. Do not believe any man who professes to give it you. If he tells you some legend of a god who taught the Wheat-eating Race, the Ploughers, and the Lords to make cheese, tell him such tales are true symbols, but symbols only. If he tells you that cheese was an evolution and a development, oh! then!--bring up your guns! Open on the fellow and sweep his intolerable lack of intelligence from the earth. Ask him if he

7

discovers reality to be a function of time, and Being to hide in clockwork. Keep him on the hop with ironical comments upon how it may be that environment can act upon Will, while Will can do nothing with environment--whose proper name is mud. Pester the provincial. Run him off the field.

But about cheese. Its noble antiquity breeds in it a noble diffusion.

This happy Christendom of ours (which is just now suffering from an indigestion and needs a doctor--but having also a complication of insomnia cannot recollect his name) has been multifarious incredibly--but in nothing more than in cheese!

One cheese differs from another, and the difference is in sweeps, and in landscapes, and in provinces, and in countrysides, and in climates, and in principalities, and in realms, and in the nature of things. Cheese does most gloriously reflect the multitudinous effect of earthly things, which could not be multitudinous did they not proceed from one mind.

Consider the cheese of Rocquefort: how hard it is in its little box. Consider the cheese of Camembert, which is hard also, and also lives in a little box, but must not be eaten until it is soft and yellow. Consider the cheese of Stilton, which is not made there, and of Cheddar, which is. Then there is your Parmesan, which idiots buy rancid in bottles, but which the wise grate daily for their use: you think it is hard from its birth? You are mistaken. It is the world that hardens the Parmesan. In its youth the Parmesan is very soft and easy, and is voraciously devoured.

Then there is your cheese of Wensleydale, which is made in Wensleydale, and your little Swiss cheese, which is soft and creamy and eaten with sugar, and there is your Cheshire cheese and your little Cornish cheese, whose name escapes me, and your huge round cheese out of the Midlands, as big as a fort whose name I never heard. There is your toasted or Welsh cheese, and your cheese of Pont-l'evêque, and your white cheese of Brie, which is a chalky sort of cheese. And there is your cheese of Neufchatel, and there is your Gorgonzola cheese, which is mottled all over like some marbles, or like that Mediterranean soap which is made of wood-ash and of olive oil. There is your Gloucester cheese called the Double Gloucester, and I have read in a book of Dunlop cheese, which is made in Ayrshire: they could tell you more about it in Kilmarnock. Then Suffolk makes a cheese, but does not give it any name; and talking of that reminds me how going to Le Quesnoy to pass the people there the time of day, and to see what was left of that famous but forgotten fortress, a young man there showed me a cheese, which he told me also had no name, but which was native to the town, and in the valley of Ste. Engrace, where is that great wood which shuts off all the world, they make their cheese of ewe's milk and sell it in Tardets, which is their only livelihood. They make a cheese in Port-Salut which is a very subtle cheese, and there is a cheese of Limburg, and I know not how many others, or rather I know them, but you have had enough: for a little cheese goes a long way. No man is a glutton on cheese.

What other cheese has great holes in it like Gruyere, or what other is as round as a cannon-ball like that cheese called Dutch? which reminds me:--

Talking of Dutch cheese. Do you not notice how the intimate mind of Europe is reflected in cheese? For in the centre of Europe, and where Europe is most active, I mean in Britain and in Gaul and in Northern Italy, and in the valley of the Rhine--nay, to some extent in Spain (in her Pyrenean valleys at least)--there flourishes a vast burgeoning of cheese, infinite in variety, one in goodness. But as Europe fades away under the African wound which Spain suffered or the Eastern barbarism of the Elbe, what happens to cheese? It becomes very flat and similar. You can quote six cheeses perhaps which the public power of Christendom has founded outside the limits of its ancient Empire--but not more than six. I will quote you 253 between the Ebro and the Grampians, between Brindisi and the Irish Channel.

I do not write vainly. It is a profound thing.

The Captain of Industry

The heir of the merchant Mahmoud had not disappointed that great financier while he still lived, and when he died he had the satisfaction of seeing the young man, now twenty-five years of age, successfully conducting his numerous affairs, and increasing (fabulous as this may seem) the millions with which his uncle entrusted him.

Shortly after Mahmoud's death the prosperity of the firm had already given rise to a new proverb, and men said: "Do you think I am Mahmoud's-Nephew?" when they were asked to lend money or in some other way to jeopardize a few coppers in the service of God or their neighbour.

It was also a current expression, "He's rich as Mahmoud's-Nephew," when comrades would jest against some young fellow who was flusher than usual, and could afford a quart or even a gallon of wine for the company; while again the discontented and the oppressed would mutter between their teeth: "Heaven will take vengeance at last upon these Mahmoud's-Nephews!" In a word, "Mahmoud's-Nephew" came to mean throughout the whole Caliphate and wherever the True Believers spread their empire, an exceedingly wealthy man. But Mahmoud himself having been dead ten years and his heir the fortunate head of the establishment being now well over thirty years of age, there happened a very inexplicable and outrageous accident: he died--and after his death no instructions were discovered as to what should be done with this enormous capital, no will could be found, and it happened moreover to be a moment of great financial delicacy when the manager of each department in the business needed all the credit he could get.

In such a quandary the Chief Organizer and confidential friend, Ahmed, upon whom the business already largely depended, and who was so circumstanced that he could draw almost at will upon the balances, imagined a most intelligent way of escaping from the difficulties that would arise when the death of the principal was known.

He caused a quantity of hay, of straw, of dust and of other worthless materials to be stuffed into a figure of canvas; this he wrapped round with the usual clothes that Mahmoud's-Nephew had worn in the office, he shrouded the face with the hood which his chief had commonly worn during life, and having so dressed the lay figure and secretly buried the real body, he admitted upon the morning after the death those who first had business with his master.

He met them at the door with smiles and bows, saying: "You know, gentlemen, that like most really successful men, my chief is as silent as his decisions are rapid; he will listen to what you have to say, and it will be a plain yes or no at the end of it."

These gentlemen came with a proposal to sell to the firm for the sum of one million dinars a barren rock in the Indian Sea, which was not even theirs, and on which indeed not one of them had ever set eyes. Their claim to advance so original a proposal was that to their certain knowledge two thousand of the wealthiest citizens of their town were willing to buy the rock again at a profit from whoever should be its possessor during the next few weeks in the fond hope of selling it once again to provincials, clerics, widows, orphans, and in general the uninstructed and the credulous--among whom had been industriously spread the report that the rock in question consisted of one solid and flawless diamond.

These gentlemen sitting round the table before the shrouded figure laid down their proposals, whereupon the manager briefly summed up what they had said, and having done so, replied: "Gentlemen, his lordship is a man of few words; but you will have your answer in a moment if you will be good enough to rise, as he is at this moment expecting a deputation from the Holy Men who are entreating him to provide the cost of a mosque in one of the suburbs."

The proposers of the bargain rose, greatly awed and pleased by the silence and dignity of the financier who apparently remained for a moment discussing their proposals without gesture and in a tone too low for them to hear, while his manager bent over to listen.

"It is ever so," said one of them, "you may ever know the greatest men by their silence."

"You are right," said another, "he is not one to be easily deceived."

The manager in a moment or two rejoined them at the door. "Gentlemen," he said, smiling, "my chief has heard your arguments and has expressed his assent to your conditions."

They went out, delighted at the success of their mission, and congratulated Ahmed upon the financier's genius.

"He does not," said the manager, laughing in hearty agreement, "bestow himself as a present upon all and sundry. Nor is he often caught indulging in short bouts of sleep, nor are flies diabolically left to repose undisturbed upon his features--but you must excuse me, I hear the Holy Men," and indeed from the inner room came a noise of speechifying in that doleful sing-song which is associated in Bagdad with the practice of religion.

The gentlemen who had thus had the luck to interview

11

Mahmoud's-Nephew with such success in the matter of the Diamond Island, soon spread about the news, and confirmed their fellow-citizens in the certitude that a great financier is neither talkative nor vivacious. "Still waters run deep," they said, and all those to whom they said it nodded in a wise acquiescence. Nor had the Manager the least difficulty in receiving one set of customers after another and in negotiating within three weeks an infinite amount of business, all of which confirmed those who had the pleasure of an audience with the stuffed dummy that great fortunes were made and retained by reticence and a contempt for convivial weakness.

At last the ingenious man of affairs, to whom the whole combination was due, was not a little disturbed to receive from the Caliph a note couched in the following terms:

"The Commander of the Faithful and the Servant of the Merciful whose name be exalted, to the Nephew of Mahmoud:

"My Lord:--

"It has been the custom since the days of my grandfather (May his soul see God!) for the more wealthy of the Faithful to be called to my councils, and upon my summoning them thither it has not been unusual for them to present sums varying in magnitude but always proportionate to their total fortunes. My court will receive signal honour if you will present yourself after the morning prayer of the day after to-morrow. My treasurer will receive from you with gratitude and remembrance upon the previous day and not later than noon, the sum of one million dinars."

Here, indeed, was a perplexity. The payment of the money was an easy matter and was duly accomplished; but how should the lay figure which did duty in such domestic scenes as the negotiation of loans, the bullying of debtors, the purchase of options, and the cheating of the innocent and the embarrassed, take his place in the Caliph's council and remain undiscovered? For great as was the reputation of Mahmoud's-Nephew for discretion and for golden silence, such as are proper to the accumulation of great wealth, there would seem a necessity in any political assembly to open the mouth from time to time, if only for the giving of a vote.

But Ahmed, who had by this time accumulated into his own hands the millions formerly his master's, finally solved the problem. Judicious presents to the servants of the palace and the public criers made his way the easier, and on the summoning of the council Mahmoud's-Nephew, whose troublesome affection of the throat was now publicly discussed, was permitted to bring into the council-room his private secretary and manager.

Moreover at the council, as at his private office, the continued taciturnity of the millionaire could not but impress the politicians as it had already impressed the financial world.

"He does not waste his breath in tub-thumping," said one, looking reverently at the sealed figure.

"No," another would reply, "they may ridicule our old-fashioned, honest, quiet Mohammedan country gentlemen, but for common sense I will back them against all the brilliant paradoxical young fellows of our day."

"They say he is very kind at heart and lovable," a third would then add, upon which a fourth would bear his testimony thus:

"Yes, and though he says nothing about it, his charitable gifts are enormous."

By the second meeting of the council the lay figure had achieved a reputation of so high a sort that the Caliph himself insisted upon making him a domestic adviser, one of the three who perpetually associated with the Commander of the Faithful and directed his policy. For the universal esteem in which the new councillor was held had affected that Prince very deeply.

Here there arose a crux from which there could be no escape, as one of the three chief councillors, Mahmoud's-Nephew, must speak at last and deliver judgments!

The Manager, first considering the whole business, and next adding up his private gains, which he had carefully laid out in estates of which the firm and its employés knew nothing, decided that he could afford to retire. What might happen to the general business after his withdrawal would not be his concern.

He first gave out, therefore, that the millionaire was taken exceedingly ill, and that his life was despaired of: later, within a few hours, that he was dead.

So far from attempting to allay the panic which ensued, Ahmed frankly admitted the worst.

With cries of despair and a confident appeal to the justice of Heaven against such intrigues, the honest fellow permitted the whole of the vast business to be wound up in favour of newcomers, who had not forgotten to reward him, and soothing as best he could the ruined crowds of small investors who thronged round him for help and advice, he retired under an assumed name to his highly profitable estates, which were situated in the most distant provinces of the known world.

As for Mahmoud's-Nephew, three theories arose about him which are still disputed to this day:

The first was that his magnificent brain with its equitable judgment and its power of strict secrecy, had designed plans too far advanced for his time, and that his bankruptcy was due to excess of wisdom.

The second theory would have it that by "going into politics" (as the phrase runs in Bagdad) he had dissipated his energies, neglected his business, and that the inevitable consequences had followed.

The third theory was far more reasonable. Mahmoud's-Nephew, according to this, had towards the end of his life lost judgment; his garrulous indecision within the last few days before his death was notorious: in the Caliph's council, as those who should best know were sure, one could hardly get a word in edgewise for his bombastic self-assurance; while in matters of business, to conduct a bargain with him was more like attending a public meeting than the prosecution of negotiations with a respectable banker.

In a word, it was generally agreed that Mahmoud's-Nephew's success had been bound up with his splendid silence, his fall, bankruptcy, and death, with a lesion of the brain which had disturbed this miracle of self-control.

The Inventor

I had a day free between two lectures in the south-west of England, and I spent it stopping at a town in which there was a large and very comfortable old posting-house or coaching-inn. I had meant to stay some few hours there and to take the last train out in the evening, and I had meant to spend those hours alone and resting; but this was not permitted me, for just as I had taken up the local paper, which was a humble, reasonable thing, empty of any passion and violence and very reposeful to read, a man came up and touched my left elbow sharply: a gesture not at all to my taste nor, I think, to that of anyone who is trying to read his paper.

I looked up and saw a man who must have been quite sixty years of age. He had on a soft, felt slouch hat, a very old and greenish black coat; he stooped and shuffled; he was clean-shaven, with long grey hair, and his eyes were astonishingly bright and piercing and set close together.

He said, "I beg your pardon."

I said, "Eh, what?"

He said again "I beg your pardon" in the tones of a man who almost commands, and having said this he put his hat on the table, dragged a chair quite close to mine, and pulled a folded bunch of foolscap sheets out of his pocket. His manner was that of a man who engages your attention and has a right to engage it. There were no preliminaries and there was no introduction. This was apparently his manner, and I submitted.

"I have here," he said, fixing me with his intense eyes, "the plans for a speedometer."

"Oh!" said I.

"You know what a speedometer is?" he asked suspiciously.

I said yes. I said it was a machine for measuring the speed of vehicles, and that it was compounded of two (or more) Greek words.

He nodded; he was pleased that I knew so much, and could therefore listen to his tale and understand it. He pulled his grey baggy trousers up over the knee, settled himself, sitting forward, and opened his document. He cleared his throat, still fixing me with those eyes of his, and said--

"Every speedometer up to now has depended upon the same principle as a Watt's governor; that is, there are two little balls attached to each by a limb to a central shaft: they rise and fall according to their speed of rotation, and this movement is indicated upon a dial."

I nodded.

He cleared his throat again. "Of course, that is unsatisfactory."

"Damnably!" said I, but this reply did not check him.

"It works tolerably well at high speeds; at low speeds it is useless; and then again there is a very rapid fluctuation, and the instrument is of only approximate precision."

"Not it!" said I to encourage him.

"There is one exception," he continued, "to this principle, and that is a speedometer which depends upon the introduction of resistance into a current generated by a small magneto. The faster the magneto turns the stronger the current generated, and the change is indicated upon a dial."

"Yes," said I sadly, "as in the former case so in this; the change of speed is indicated upon a dial." And I sighed.

"But this method also," he went on tenaciously, "has its defects."

"You may lay to that," I interrupted.

"It has the defect that at high speeds its readings are not quite correct, and at very low speeds still less so. Moreover, it is said that it slightly deteriorates with the passage of time."

"Now that," I broke in emphatically, "is a defect I have discovered in----"

But he put up his hand to stop me. "It slightly deteriorates, I say, with the passage of time." He paused a moment impressively. "No one has hitherto discovered any system which will accurately record the speed of a vehicle or of any rotary movement and register it at the lowest as at the highest speeds." He paused again for a still longer period in order to give still greater emphasis to what he had to say. He concluded in a new note of sober triumph: "I have solved the problem!"

I thought this was the end of him, and I got up and beamed a congratulation at him and asked if he would drink anything, but he only said, "Please sit down again and I will explain."

There is no way of combating this sort of thing, and so I sat down, and he went on:

"It is perfectly simple...." He passed his hand over his forehead. "It is so simple that one would say it must have been thought of before; but that is what is always said of a great invention.... Now I have here" (and he opened out his foolscap) "the full details. But I will not read them to you; I will summarize them briefly."

"Have you a plan or anything I could watch?" said I a little anxiously.

"No," he answered sharply, "I have not, but if you like I will

16

draw a rough sketch as I go along upon the margin of your newspaper."

"Thank you," I said.

He drew the newspaper towards him and put it on his knee. He pulled out a pencil; he held the foolscap up before his eye, and he began to describe.

"The general principle upon which my speedometer reposes," he said solemnly, "is the coordination of the cylinder and the cone upon an angle which will have to be determined in practice, and will probably vary for different types. But it will never fall below 15 nor rise over 43."

"I should have thought----" I began, but he told me I could not yet have grasped it, and that he wished to be more explicit.

"On a king bolt," he said, occasionally consulting his notes, "runs a pivot in bevel which is kept in place by a small hair-spring, which spring fits loosely on the Conkling Shaft."

"Exactly," said I, "I see what is coming."

But he wouldn't let me off so easily.

"Yes, of course you are going to say that the whole will be keyed together, and that the T-pattern nuts on a movable shank will be my method of attachment to the fixed portion next to the cam? Eh? So it is, but" (and here his eye brightened), "anyone could have arranged that. My particularity is that I have a freedom of movement even at the lowest speeds, and an accuracy of notation even at the highest, which is secured in a wholly novel manner ... and yet so simply. What do you think it is?"

I affected to look puzzled, and thought for a moment. "I cannot imagine," said I, "unless----"

"No," he interrupted, "do not try to guess it, for you never will. I turn the flange inward on a Wilkinson lathe and give it a parabolic section so that the axes are always parallel to each other and to the shaft.... There!"

I had no idea the man could be so moved: there was jubilation in his voice.

"There!" he said again, as though some effort of the brain had exhausted him. "It can't be touched, mind you," he added suspiciously; "I've taken out the provisional patents. There's one man I know wants to fight it in the courts as an infringement on Wilkinson's own patent, but it can't be touched!" He shook his head decisively. "No! my lawyer's certain of that--and so'm I!"

Here there was a break in his communications, so to speak, and he had apparently run out. It was not for me to wind him up again. I watched him with a sombre relief as he stood up again to full height, leaned his head back, and sighed profoundly with

17

satisfaction and with completion. He folded up his specification and put it in his pocket again. He tore off the incomprehensible sketch he had made with his pencil while he was speaking, and put it by me on the mantelshelf. "You might like to keep it," he said pathetically; "it's a document, that is; it will be famous some day." He looked at it lovingly, almost as though he was going to take it back again: but he thought better of it.

I was waiting, I will not say itching, for him to take his leave, when a god or demon, that same perhaps which had treated the poor fellow as a jest for a whole lifetime, inspired him to take a very false step indeed. He had already taken up his hat and was turning as though to go to the door, when the unfortunate thought struck him.

"What would you do?" he said.

"How do you mean?" I answered.

"Why, what would you do to try and get it taken up and talked about?"

Then it was my turn, and I let him have it.

"You must get the Press and the Government to work together," I said rapidly, "and particularly in connection with the new Government Service of Camion's Fettle-Trains and Cursory Circuits."

He nodded like one who thoroughly understands and desires to hear more.

"Speed," I added nonchalantly, "and the measure of it are of course essentials in their case."

He nodded again.

"And they have never really settled the problem ... especially about Fettle-Trains."

"No," said he ponderously, "so I understand."

"Well now," I went on, full of the chase, "you will naturally ask me who are you to go to?" I scratched my nose. "You know the Fusionary Office, as we call it? It is really, of course, a part of the Stannaries. But the Chief Permanent Secretary likes to have it called the Fusionary Office; it's his vanity."

"Yes," said he eagerly, "yes, go on!"

"They always have the same hours," I said, "four to eleven."

"Four to what?" he asked, looking up.

"To eleven," I repeated sharply; "but you'd much better call round about three."

He looked bewildered.

"Don't interrupt," I said, seeing him open his lips, "or I shall lose the thread. It's rather complicated. You call at three by the little

18

door in Whitehall on the Embankment side towards the Horse Guards looking south, and don't ring the bell."

"Why not?" he asked. I thought for the moment he might begin to cry.

"Oh, well," I said testily, "you mustn't ask those questions. All these institutions are very old institutions with habits and prejudices of their own. You mustn't ring the bell, that's all; they don't like it; you must just wait until they open; and then, if you take my advice, don't write a note or ask to interview the First Analyist. Don't do any of the usual things, but just fill up one of the regular Treasury forms and state that you have come with regard to the Perception and Mensuration advertisements."

His face was pained and wrinkled as he heard me, but he said, "I beg your pardon ... but shall I have it all explained to me at the office?"

"Certainly not!" I said, aghast; "it's just because you might have so much difficulty there that I'm explaining everything to you."

"Yes, I know," he said doubtfully; "thank you."

"I hope you'll try and follow what I say," I continued a little wearily; "I have special opportunities for knowing.... Political, you know."

"Certainly," he said, "certainly; but about those forms?"

"Well," I said, "you didn't suppose they supplied them, did you?"

"I almost did," he ventured.

"Oh, you did," said I, with a loud laugh, "well, you're wrong there. However, I dare say I've got one on me." He looked up eagerly as I felt in my pockets. I brought out a telegraph blank, two letters, and a tobacco pouch. I looked at them for a moment. "No," said I, "I haven't got one; it's a pity, but I'll tell you who will give you one; you know the place opposite, where the bills are drafted?"

"I'm afraid I don't," he said, admitting ignorance for the first time in this conversation and perhaps in his life.

"Well," said I impatiently, "never mind, anyone will show you. Go there, and if they don't give you a form they'll show you a copy of Paper B, which is much the same thing."

"Thank you," said he humbly, and he got up to move out. He was going a little groggily, his eyes were dull and sodden. He presented all the aspect of a man under a heavy strain.

"You've got it all clear, I hope?" I asked cheerfully as he neared the door.

"Oh, yes!" he said. "Thank you; yes!"

"Anything else?" I shouted as he passed out into the courtyard. "Anything else I can do? You'll always find me in the

19

room over the office, Room H, down the little iron staircase," I nodded genially to him as he disappeared.

In this way did we exchange, the Inventor and I, those expert confidences and mutual aids in either's technical skill which are too rarely discovered in modern travel.

The Views of England

England is a country with edges and with a core. It is a country very small for the number of people who live in it, and very appreciable to the eye for the traveller who travels on foot or in a boat from place to place. Considering the part it has in the making of the world, it might justly be compared to a jewel which is very small and very valuable and can almost be held in the hand. The physical appreciation of England is to be reached by an appreciation of landscape.

It so happens that England is traversed by remarkable and sudden ranges; hills with a sharp escarpment overlooking great undulating plains. This is not true of any other one country of Europe, but it is true of England, and a man who professes to consider, to understand, to criticize, to defend, and to love this country, must know the Pennines, the Cotswolds, the North and the South Downs, the Chilterns, the Mendips, and the Malverns; he must know Delamere Forest, and he must know the Hill of Beeston, from which all Cheshire may be perceived. If he knows these heights and has long considered the prospects which they afford, he can claim to have seen the face of England.

It is deplorable that our modern method of travel does cut us off from such experiences. They were not only common to, they were necessary to our fathers; the roads would not be at the expense of tunnelling through hills, and (what is more important) when those men who most mould the knowledge of the country by the country (the people who deal with its soil, who live separate upon its separate farms) visited each other upon horses; and horses, unlike railway trains, cannot climb hills. They puff, they heave, they snort, as do railway trains, but they climb them well.

On this account, because the roads for the carriages went over hills, and because the method of visiting even a near neighbour would permit you to go over hills, the England of quite a little time ago was familiar with the half-dozen great landscapes of England. You may see it in that most individual, that most peculiar, and, I think, that most glorious school of painters, the English landscape painter, Constable with his thick colours, Turner with his wonderment, and even the portrait painters in their backgrounds depend upon the view of the plains from a height. To-day our landscape painters sometimes do the same, but the market for that emotion is capricious, it is no longer the secure and natural way of presenting England to English eyes.

21

If you will consider these plains at the foot of the English hills you will find in them the whole history of the country, and the whole meaning of it as well. Two occur to me first: The view of the Weald (both Kentish and Sussex) through which the influence of Europe perpetually approached the island, not only in the crisis of the Roman or the Norman invasions, but in a hundred episodes stretched out through two thousand years--and the view of the Thames Valley as one gets it on a clear day from the summits of the North Downs when one looks northward and sees very faintly the Chilterns along the horizon.

This last is obscured by London. One needs a very particular circumstance in which to appreciate it. The air must be dry and clear, there must be little or no wind, or if there is a wind it must be a strong one from the south and west that has already driven the smoke from the western edge of the town. When this is so, a man looks right across to the sandy heights just north of the Thames, and far beyond he sees the Chilterns, like a landfall upon the rim of the world. He looks at all that soil on which the government of this country has been rooted. He sees the hill of Windsor. He overlooks, though he cannot perceive at so great a distance, the two great schools of the rich; he has within one view the principal Castle of the Kings, the place of their council, and the cathedral of their capital city: so true is it that the Thames made England.

Then, if you consider the upper half of that valley, the view is from the ridge of the Berkshire hills, or, better still, from Cumnor, or from the clump of trees above Faringdon. From such look-outs the astonishing loneliness which England has had the strength to preserve in this historic belt of land profoundly strikes a man. You can see to your left and, a long way off, the hill where, as is most probable, Alfred thrust back the Pagans, and so saved one-half of Christendom. Oxford is within your landscape. The roll upwards in a glacis of the Cotswold, the nodal point of the Roman roads at Cirencester, and the ancient crossings of the Thames.

From the Cotswold again westward you look over a sheer wall and see one of those differences which make up England. For the passage from the Upper Thames to the flat and luxuriant valley floor of the Severn is a transition (if it be made by crossing the hills) more sudden than that between many countries abroad. Had our feudalism cut England into provinces we should here have two marked provincial histories marching together, for the natural contrast is greater than between Normandy and Brittany at any part of their march or between Aragon and Castile at any part of theirs. I do not know what it is, but the view of the jagged Malvern seen above the happy mists of autumn, when these mists lie like a warm fleece upon the orchards of the vale, preserving them of a morning until the strengthening of the sun, the sudden aspect, I say, of those jagged peaks strikes one like a vision of a new world. How many men have thought it! How often it ought to be written down! It hangs in the memory of the traveller like a permanent benediction, and remains in his mind a standing symbol of peace.

I have no space to speak of how from Beeston you see all Cheshire; the Vale Royal to your left, and the main plain of the county to your right. The whole stretch is framed in with definite hills, the last and highly marked line of the Pennines bounds the view upon the east; upon the west the first of the Welsh hills stands sharply in a long even line against the fading sun; and on the north you see the height of Delamere. There are three other views in the North of England, the first easy, the last two difficult to obtain, all between them making up a true picture of what the North of England is. The first (and it is very famous) is the view over the industrial ferment of South Lancashire, seen from the complete silence of the hills round the Peak. No matter where you cross that summit, even if you take the high road from the Snake Inn to Glossop, where the easiest, and therefore the least striking, passage has been chosen, much more if you follow the wild heights a little to the south until you come to a more abrupt descent on which there are not even paths, there comes a point where there is presented to you in one great offering, without introduction, a vision of the vast energies of England.

I remember once in winter when the sun sets early (it was December, and seven years ago) coming upon this sight. The clouds were so arranged after an Atlantic storm that all the heaven (which here is always spacious and noble) was covered with a rolling curtain as though a man had pulled it with his hands. But far off, westward, there was a broad red band of sunset, and against this the smoke, the tall stacks, the violence and the wealth of that cauldron. One could almost hear the noise. It did arrest one; it was as though someone had painted something unreal, to be a mystical emblem, and to sum up in one picture all those million despairs, misfortunes, chances, disciplines, and acquirements which make up the character of Lancashire men. This vision also many men have seen and many men shall write of. Very rarely upon the surface of the earth does the soul take on so immediate and obvious a physical body as does the soul of that industrial world in the view of which I speak.

And the two other views are, first, that difficult one which one must pick and choose but which can be obtained from several sites (especially at the end of Wensleydale), and which is the view of that rich, old, and agricultural Yorkshire, from which the county draws its traditions and in which, perhaps, the truest spirit of the county still abides; for Yorkshire is at heart farmer, and possibly after three generations of a town, a man from this part of England still looks more lively when he sees a lively horse put before him for judgment. Second, the view from Cross Fell, very, very difficult to obtain, for often when one climbs Cross Fell in sunny weather, one gets up over the Scar under the threat of cloud, and one only reaches the summit by the time the evening or the mist has fallen; but if one has the luck to see the view of which I speak, then one sees all that rugged remaining part of the Northwest exactly as the Romans saw it, and as it has been for two thousand years, with the high land of the lakes and the stony nature and the sparseness of all the stretch about one, and the approach to a foreign land.

I have often thought when I have heard men blaming the story of England or her present mood for false reasons, or, what is worse, praising her for false reasons; when I have heard the men of the cities talking wild talk got from maps and from print, or the disappointed men talking wild talk of another kind, expecting impossible or foreign perfections from their own kindred--I have often thought, I say, when I have heard the folly upon either side (and the mass of it daily increases)--that it would be a wholesome thing if one could take such a talker and make him walk from Dover to the Solway, exercising some care that he should rise before the sun, and that he should see in clear weather the views of which I speak. A man who has done that has seen England--not the name or the map or the rhetorical catchword, but the thing. And it does not take so very long.

The Lunatic

Those who are interested in what simple straightforward people call the Pathology of Consciousness have gathered a great body of evidence upon the various manias that affect men, and there is an especially interesting department of this which concerns illusion upon matters which in the sane are determinable by the senses and common experience. Thus one man will believe himself to be the Emperor of China, another to be William Shakespeare or some other impossible person, though one would imagine that his every accident of daily life would convince him to the contrary.

I had recently occasion to watch one of the most harmless and yet one of the most striking of these illusions in a private asylum which has specialized, if I may so express myself, upon men of letters. The case was harmless and even benign, for the poor fellow was not of a combative disposition to begin with, was of too careful and dignified a temperament to show more than slight irritation if his delusion were contradicted. This misfortune, however, very rarely overtook him, for those who came to visit him were warned to humour his whim. This eccentricity I will now describe.

He imagined, nay he was convinced, that he was existing fifty years in the future, and that the interest of his conversation for others would lie in his reminiscence of the state of society in which we are actually living today. If anyone who had not been warned was imprudent enough to suggest that the conversation was taking place in 1909 would smile gently, nod, and say rather bitterly, "Yes, I know, I know," as though recognizing a universal plot against him which he was too weary to combat. But when he had said this he would continue to talk on as though both parties to the conversation were equally convinced that the year was really 1960 or thereabouts. Whether to add zest to what he said or from some part of his malady consonant with all the rest, my poor friend (who had been a journalist and will very possibly be a journalist again) presupposed that the whole structure of society as we now know it had changed and that his reminiscences were those of a past time which, on account of some great revolution or other, men imperfectly comprehended, so that it must be of the highest interest and advantage to listen to the testimony of an eye-witness upon them.

What especially delighted him (for he was a zealous admirer of the society he described) was the method of government.

"There was no possibility of going wrong," he said to me with curious zeal, "not a shadow of danger! It would be difficult for you to understand now how easily the system worked!" And here he sighed profoundly. "And why on earth," he continued, "men should have destroyed such an instrument when they had it is more than I can understand. There it was in every country in Europe; there were elections; all the men voted. And mind you, the elections were not so very far apart. Most people living at one election could remember the last, so there was no time for abuses to spring up.... Well, everybody voted. If a man wanted one thing he voted one way, and if he wanted another thing he voted the other way. The people for whom he voted would then meet, and with a sense of duty which I cannot exaggerate they would work month after month exactly to reproduce the will of those who had appointed them. It was a great time!"

"Yet," said I, "even so there must have been occasional divergences between what these people did and what the nation wanted."

"I see what you mean," he said, musing, "you mean that all the devotion in the world, the purest of motives and the most devoted sense of duty, could not keep the elected always in contact with the electors. You are right. But you must remember that in every country there was a machinery, with regard to the most important measures at least, which could throw the matter before the electors to be re-decided. I can remember no important occasion upon which the machinery was not brought into use."

"But, after all, the value of the decisions of the electorate you are describing," said I, continuing to humour him, "would depend upon the information which the electorate had received as well as upon their judgment."

"As for their judgment," he said, a little shortly, "it is not for our time to criticize theirs. Human judgment is not infallible, but I can well remember how in every nation of Europe it was the fixed conviction of the citizens that judgment was their chief characteristic, and especially judgment in national affairs. I cannot believe that so universal an attitude of the mind could have arisen had it not been justified. But as for information, they had the Press ... a free Press!" Here he fell into a reverie, so powerfully did his supposed memories affect him.

I was willing to lead him on, because this kind of illness is best met by sympathy, and also because I was not uninterested to discover how his own trade had affected him.

"You would hardly understand it," he said sadly; "what you hear from me is nothing but words.... I wish I could have shown you one of those great houses with information pouring in as rapid, as light, and as clear, from every hidden corner of the world, digested by master brains into the most lucid and terse presentment of it possible, and then whirled out on great wheels to be distributed by the thousand and the hundred thousand, to the hungry intelligence of Europe. There was nothing escaped it--nothing. In every capital were crowds of men dispatched from the other capitals of our civilization, moving with ease in the wealthiest houses, and exquisitely in touch with the most delicate phases of national life everywhere. And these men were such experts in selection that a picture of Europe as a whole was presented every morning to each particular part of Europe; and nowhere was this more successfully accomplished than in my own beloved town of London."

"It must have been useful," I said, "not only for the political purposes you describe, but also for investors. Indeed, I should imagine that the two things ran together." "You are right," he said with interest, "the wide knowledge which even the poorest of the people possessed upon foreign affairs, through the action of the Press, was, further, of the utmost and most beneficent effect in teaching even the smallest proprietor what he need do with his capital. A discovery of metallic ore--especially of gold--a new invention, anything which might require development, was at once presented in its most exact aspect to the reader."

"It was probably upon that account," said I, "that property was so equally distributed, and that so general a prosperity reigned as you have often described to me."

"You are right," said he; "it was mainly this accurate and universal daily information which produced such excellent results."

"But it occurs to me," said I, by way of stimulating his conversation with an objection, "that if so passionate and tenacious a habit of telling the exact truth upon innumerable things was present in this old institution of which you speak, it cannot but have bred a certain amount of dissension, and it must sometimes even have done definite harm to individuals whose private actions were thus exposed."

"You are right," said he; "the danger of such misfortunes was always present, and with the greatest desire in the world to support only what was worthy the writers of the journals of which I speak would occasionally blunder against private interests; but there was a remedy."

"What was that?" I asked.

"Why, the law provided that in this matter twelve men called a jury, instructed by a judge, after the matter had been fully explained to them by two other men whose business it was to examine the truth boldly for the sake of justice--I say the law provided that the twelve men after this process should decide whether the person injured should receive money from the newspaper or no, and if so, in what amount. And, lest there should still be any manner of doubt, the judge was permitted to set aside their verdict if he thought it unjust. To secure his absolute impartiality as between rich and poor he was paid somewhat over £100 a week, a large salary in those days, and he was further granted the right of imprisoning people at will or of taking away their property if he believed them to obstruct his judgment. Nor were these the only safeguards. For in the case of very rich men, to whom justice might not be done on account of the natural envy of their poorer fellow-citizens, it was arranged that the jury should consist only of rich men. In this way it was absolutely certain that a complete impartiality would reign. We shall never see those days again," he concluded.

"But do you not think," I said before I left him, "that the social perfection of the kind you have described must rather have been due to some spirit of the time than to particular institutions? For after all the zealous love of justice and the sense of duty which you describe are not social elements to be produced by laws."

"Possibly," he said, wearily, "possibly, but we shall never see it again!"

And I left him looking into the fire with infinite sadness and reflecting upon his lost youth and the year 1909: a pathetic figure, and one whose upkeep during the period of his deficiency was a very serious drain upon the resources of his family.

The Inheritance of Humour

There are some truths which seem to get old almost as soon as they are born, and that simply because they are so astonishingly true that people soon get to feel as though they have known them all their lives; and such a truth is that which first one writer and then another in the last five years has been insisting upon, until it is already a perfect commonplace that nations do not know their own qualities. The inmost, the characteristic thing, that which differentiates one community from another, as tastes or colours differentiate things--that a nation hardly ever knows until it is pointed out to it by some foreigner or by some observer from within. It cannot know it, because one cannot tell the very atmosphere in which one lives. It is universal and therefore unnoticed. Now, if this is true of any nation, it is particularly true of England. And English people need to be told morning, noon, and night, not indeed the particular national characteristic which they have, since for this no particular name could be found, but rather what its evidences are; as, for instance, spontaneity in design, a passion for the mystical in poetry and the arts; a power in water-colour, in which they are perhaps quite alone, and certainly the first in Europe; and, above all, the chief, the master thing of all, humour.

There is not nor ever will be anything like English humour. It is a thing quite apart, and by it for now more than two hundred years you may know England. It does not puzzle the foreigner (as the more blatant kind of intellectual man is too fond of boasting that it does); he simply admires it as a rule and wonders at it always; sometimes he actually dislikes it, but by it he knows that the thing he is reading is English and has the savour and taste of England.

It is impossible to define it, because it is so full of stuff and so organic a quality; but in our own time it was principally the pencil of Charles Keene that has summed it up and presented it in a moment and at once to the eye--the pencil of Charles Keene and that profound instinct whereby he chose the legends for his drawing, whether he found them by his own sympathy with the people or whether they were suggested to him by friends.

It is the verdict of the men most competent perhaps to judge upon these things that he had the greatest graphic power of his time, and that no one had had that power to such an extent since Hogarth. Upon these things the men of the trade must dispute; the layman cannot doubt that he had here a genius and a genius comprehensively national. It is the essence of a good draughtsman that what he wants to draw, that he draws. The line that he desires to see upon the paper appears there as his fingers move. It is a quality extremely rare in its perfection. And Charles Keene had it in perfection, as in totally different manner had the offensive and diseased talent of Beardsley.

But more important than the power to do is the quality of the thing done, and the work of Charles Keene, multitudinous, varied, always great, is an inheritance for English people comparable to the inheritance they have in Dickens. It has also what Dickens had, a power of representing, as it were, the essential English. Just that which makes people say (with some truth) that Dickens never drew a gentleman would make them say with equal truth that what was interesting in the gentlemen of Charles Keene (and he perpetually drew them) was not the externals upon which gentlemen so pride themselves, but the soul. Thus I have in mind one picture wherein Keene drew a gentleman; true, he was a gentleman who had just swallowed a bad oyster, and therefore he was a man as well. I recall another of an old gentleman complaining of the caterpillar on his chop: he is a gentleman of the professional rather than the territorial classes, and, great heavens! what a power of line! All you see beneath the round of his hat is the end of his nose, the curve of his mouth, and two bushy ends of whiskers. Yet one can tell all about that man; one could write a book on him. One knows his economics, his religion, his accent, and what he thought of the Third Napoleon and what of Garibaldi. I have called draughtsmanship of this quality an inheritance--I might have called it perhaps with better propriety a monument. It is possible that England in the near future will look back with great envy, as she will certainly look back with great pride, to the generation preceding our own: they were a solid and a happy community of men. How much they owed to fortune, how much to themselves, it is not the place of such random stuff as mine to consider.

They were nearly impregnable in their island; they were not bellicose. They made and sold for all the world. Whether the very different future which we are now entering is to be laid to their door or to our own, that generation will still remain one of the principal things in English history, like the Elizabethan generation, or the group of men who organized the Seven Years' War, or the group of men who fought in the Peninsula. And of that generation the note of health and of stability is represented by its humour. I am not sure that of all things educational to young men with no personal memory of that time, and especially to young men with no family tradition of it to reflect it in their books and their furniture; and--

this yet more particularly--to young men born out of England yet claiming communion with England, the Anglo-Indians and the Colonials--I am not sure, I say, that the thing most educational to these would not be some hundred of Charles Keene's drawings, for therein they would find what it was that gave them the power and the wealth that can hardly be defended unless its traditions are continued. Note how Victorian England dealt with the humour of a Volunteer review; note how it dealt with the humour of excessive wealth; and note how it dealt with the humour of schools and of Dons. One might almost define it by negations. There is in all of it no--but here I lack a word.... When things ring false it is because they have got by exaggeration or by some other form of falsity beside themselves. Appreciation of rank or even of worth becomes snobbishness; appreciation of another's judgment false taste; and patriotism, the most beautiful, the noblest, the most necessary of the great emotions, corrupts into something very vile indeed.

Well, the Victorians, and notably this man of whose power of the pencil I am speaking, did lack that false savour, that savour of just missing what one wishes to say or to feel, which haunts us to-day; and I should imagine that whether it were cause or effect the salt present in the preservation of the moral health of that society was humour. Let us enjoy it like an heirloom. It is more national than the language; at least it is more national than what the language has become under foreign pressure; it is infinitely more national than our problems and our tragedies. It is so national that--who knows?--it may crop up again of itself one of these days; and may that not be long.

The Old Gentleman's Opinions

I had occasion about a fortnight ago to meet a man more nearly ninety than eighty years of age, who had had special opportunity for discovering the changes of Europe during his long life. He was of the English wealthier classes by lineage, but his mother had been of the French nobility and a Huguenot. His father had been prominent in the diplomacy of a couple of generations ago. He had travelled widely, read perhaps less widely, but had known and appreciated an astonishing number of his contemporaries.

I was interested (without any power of my own to judge whether his decisions were right or wrong) to discover what most struck him in the changes produced by that great stretch of years, all of which he had personally observed: he was born just after Waterloo, and he could remember the Reform Bill.

He surprised me by telling me, in the first place, that the material changes and discoveries, enormous though they were in extent, were not, in his view, the most striking. He was ready to leave it open whether these material changes were the causes of moral changes more remarkable, or merely effects concomitant with these. When I asked him what had struck him most of the great material developments, he told me the phonograph and the aeroplane among inventions; Mendel's observations in the sphere of experimental knowledge; and, in the sphere of pure theory, the breakdown of many things that had been dogmas of physical science in his early manhood.

Since I did not quite understand what he meant by this last, he gave me, after some hesitation, a few examples: That the interior of the earth was molten; that a certain limited number of elements-- not all yet isolated, but certainly few in their total--were at the base of all material forms, and were immutable; that the ultimate unit of each of these was a certain indivisible, eternal thing called the Atom; and so forth.

He assured me that views of this sort, extending over a hundred or a thousand other points, were so universally accepted in his time that to dispute them was to be ranked with the unlettered or the fantastic. I asked him if it were so in economics. He said: Yes, in England, where there was a similar dogma of Free Trade: not abroad.

When I asked him why Mendel's published experiments and the theory based upon them had so much impressed him, he said because it was almost the first attempt to apply to the speculative dogmas of biology some standard demonstrably true; and here he wandered off to explain to me why the commonly accepted views upon biology, which had so changed thought in the latter part of his life, were associated with the name of Darwin. Darwin, he assured me, had brought forward no new discovery, but only a new hypothesis, and that only a small and particular hypothesis, whereby to explain the general theory of transformism. This theory, he told me--the unbroken descent of living organisms and their physical connection with one another and with common parents-- had been a favourite idea from the beginning of history with many great thinkers, from Lucretius to Buffon and from Augustus of Hippo to Lamarck. Darwin's, the old gentleman assured me, which he had defended with infinite toil, was that the method in which this continuity of descent proceeded was by an infinitely slow process of very small changes differentiating each minute step from the one before and the one after it, and these small changes Darwin's hypothesis referred to a natural selection. Nothing else in Darwin's work, he assured me, was novel, and yet it was the one thing which subsequent research had rendered more and more doubtful. Darwin (he said) said nothing new that was also true.

At this point I was moved to contradict the old gentleman, and to say that one unquestioned contribution to science of Darwin, as novel as it was secure, was his patient discovery of the work of earthworms, and of its vast effect. The old gentleman was willing to admit that I was right, but he said he was only speaking of Darwin in connection with transformism and the whimsical way in which his private name (and his errors) had become identified with evolution in general.

I asked him, since he had such a knowledge of men from observation, why this was so.

"It seems at first sight," he said, "as ridiculous as though we should associate the theory of light with the name of Newton, who inclined to the exploded corpuscular hypothesis, or the general conception of orbital motion in the universe to the great Bacon, who, in point of fact, rudely repudiated the Copernican theory in particular."

"Did he, indeed?" said I, interested.

"I believe so," said the old gentleman; "at any rate you were asking me why Darwin, with his single contribution to the theory of transformism, and that a doubtful one--or, to be accurate, an exploded one--should be associated in the popular mind with the invention of so ancient a theory as that of evolution. The reason is, I think, no more than that he came at a particular moment when any man doing great quantities of detailed work in this field was bound to stand out exaggeratedly. The society in which he appeared had, until just before his day, accepted a narrow cosmogony, quite unknown to its ancestors. Darwin's book certainly exploded that, and the mind of his time--ignorant as it was of the past--was ready to accept the shattering of its father's idols as a new revelation."

"But you were saying," said I, when he had thus dealt harshly with a great name, "that not the material but the moral changes of your time seemed to you the greatest. Which did you mean?"

"Why, in the first place," said the old man thoughtfully and with some hesitation, "the curiously rapid decline of intelligence, or if you will have it differently, the clouding of thought that has marked the last thirty years. Men in my youth knew what they held and what they did not hold. They knew why they held it or why they did not hold it; but the attempt to enjoy the advantages of two contradictory systems at the same time, and, what is worse, the consulting of a man as an authority upon subjects he had never professed to know, are intellectual phenomena quite peculiar to the later years of my life."

I said we of the younger generation had all noticed it, as, for instance, when an honest but imperfectly intelligent chemist was listened to in his exposition of the nature of the soul, or a well-paid religious official was content to expound the consolations of Christianity while denying that Christianity was true.

"But," I continued, "we are usually told that this unfortunate decline in the express powers of the brain is due to the wide and imperfect education of the populace at the present moment."

"That is not the case," answered the old man sharply, when I had made myself clear by repeating my remarks in a louder tone, for he was a little deaf.

"That is not the case. The follies of which I speak are not particularly to be discovered among the poorer classes who have passed through the elementary schools. These" (it was to the schools that he was alluding with a comprehensive pessimism) "may account for the gross decline apparent in the public manners of our people, but not for faults which are peculiar to the upper and middle classes. It is not in the populace, but in those wealthier ranks that you will find the sort of intellectual decay of which I spoke."

I asked him whether he thought the tricks it was now considered cultured to play with mathematics came within the category of this intellectual decay. The old gentleman answered me a little abruptly that he could not judge what I was talking about.

"Why," said I, "do you believe that parallel straight lines converge or diverge?"

"Neither," said he, a little bewildered. "If they are parallel they cannot by definition either diverge or converge."

"You are, then," said I, "an old-fashioned adherent of the theory of the parabolic universe?" At which sensible reply of mine the old man muttered rather ill-temperedly, and begged me to speak of something else.

I asked him whether the knowledge of languages had not declined in his time. He said, somewhat emphatically, yes, and especially the knowledge of French, assuring me that in his early years many a Fellow of a College at Oxford or at Cambridge was capable of speaking that tongue in such a fashion as to make himself understood. On the other hand, he admitted that German and Spanish were more widely known than they had been, and Arabic certainly far more widely diffused among those officials of the Empire who took their work seriously.

When I asked him whether politics were more corrupt as time proceeded, he said No, but more cynical; and as to morals he would not judge, for he was certain that as one vice was corrected another appeared in its place.

What he told me he most deplored in the social system of his country was the power of the police and of the statistician by whom the policeman was guided. This he ascribed to the growth of great towns, to civic cowardice, and to a new taboo laid upon uniformed and labelled public authorities, who are now regarded as sacred, and also inordinately feared.

"In my youth," he said, "there was a joke that every man in Paris was known to the police. Today that is universally true, and no joke with regard to every man in London. Our movements are marked, our earnings, our expenses, and our most private affairs known to the innumerable officials of the Treasury, our records of every sort, however intimate, are exactly and correctly maintained. The obtaining of work and a livelihood is dependent upon strong organizations. There is hardly an ailment or a domestic habit, from drinking wine to eating turnips, which some crank who has obtained the ear of a politician does not control or threaten in the immediate future to control."

"As for doctors!" he began, his voice cracking with indignation, "their abominable...." but here the old gentleman fell into so violent a fit of coughing that he nearly turned black in the face, and when I respectfully slapped him on the back, in the hopes of granting him relief, he made matters worse by shaking himself at me with an energy worthy of 1842. His nurse rushed in, clapped him upon his pillows, and was prepared to vent her wrath upon me for having caused this paroxysm, when the old man's exhaustion and laboured breathing captured all her attention, and I had the opportunity to withdraw.

On Historical Evidence

The last book to be published upon the last Dauphin of France set me thinking upon what seems to me the chief practical science in which modern men should secure themselves. I mean the science of history--and in this science almost all lies in the appreciation of evidence, for one of the chief particular problems presented to the student of history at the present moment is whether the Dauphin did or did not survive his imprisonment in the Temple.

Let me first say why, to so many of us, the science of history and the appreciation of the evidence upon which it depends is of the first moment. It is because, short of vision or revelation, history is our only extension of human experience. It is true that a philosophy common to all citizens is necessary for a State if it is to, live--but short of that necessity the next most necessary factor is a knowledge of the stuff of mankind: of how men act under certain conditions and impulses. This knowledge may be acquired, and is in some measure, during the experience of one wise lifetime, but it is indefinitely extended by the accumulation of experience which history affords.

And what history so gives us is always of immediate and practical moment.

For instance, men sometimes speak with indifference of the rival theories as to the origin of European land tenure; they talk as though it were a mere academic debate whether the conception of private property in land arose comparatively late among Europeans or was native and original in our race. But you have only to watch a big popular discussion on that very great and at the present moment very living issue, the moral right to the private ownership in land, to see how heavily the historic argument weighs with every type of citizen. The instinct that gives that argument weight is a sound one, and not less sound in those who have least studied the matter than in those who have most studied it; for if our race from its immemorial origins has desired to own land as a private thing side by side with communal tenures, then it is pretty certain that we shall not modify that intention, however much we change our laws. If, on the other hand, it could be shown that before the advent of a complex civilization Europeans had no conception of private property in land, but treated land as a thing necessarily and always communal, then you could ascribe modern Socialist theories with regard to the land to that general movement of harking back to the origins which Europe has been assisting at through over a hundred years of revolution and of change.

It sounds cynical, but it is perfectly true, that much the largest factor in the historical conception of men is assertion. It is literally true that when men (with the exception of a very small proportion of scholars who are also intelligent) consider the past, the picture on which they dwell is a picture conveyed to them wholly by authority and by unquestioned authority. There was never a time when the original sources of history were more easily to be consulted by the plain man; but whether because of their very number, or because the habit is not yet formed, or because there are traditions of imaginary difficulty surrounding such reading, original sources were perhaps never less familiar to fairly educated opinion than they are today; and therefore no type of book gives more pleasure when one comes across it than those little cheap books, now becoming fairly numerous, in which the original sources, and the original sources alone, are put before the reader. Mr. Rait has already done such work in connection with Mary Queen of Scots, and Mr. Archer did it admirably in connection with the Third Crusade.

But apart from the importance of consulting original sources-- which is like hearing the very witnesses themselves in court--there is a factor in historical judgment which by some unhappy accident is peculiarly lacking in the professional historian. It is a factor to which no particular name can be attached, though it may be called a department of common sense. But it is a mental power or attitude easily recognizable in those who possess it, and perhaps atrophied by the very atmosphere of the study. It goes with the open air with a general knowledge of men and with that rapid recognition of the way in which things "fit in" which is necessarily developed by active life.

For instance, when you know the pace at which Harold marched down from the north to Hastings you recognize, if you use that factor of historic judgment of which I spake, that the affair was not barbaric. There must have been fairly good roads, and there must have been a high organization of transport. You have only to consider for a moment what a column looks like, even if it be only a brigade, to see the truth of that. Again, this type of judgment forbids anyone who uses it to ascribe great popular movements (great massacres, great turmoils, and so forth) to craft. It is a very common thing, especially in modern history, to lay such things to the power of one or two wealthy or one or two bloody leaders, but you have only to think for a few moments of what a mob is to see the falsity of that. Craft can harness this sort of explosive force, it can control it, or persuade it, or canalize it to certain issues, but it cannot create it.

38

Again, this sort of sense easily recognizes in historic types the parallels of modern experience. It avoids the error of thinking history a mistake and making of the men and women who appear there something remote from humanity, extreme, and either stilted or grandiose.

In aid of this last feature in historical judgment there is nothing of such permanent value as a portrait. Obtain your conception (as, indeed, most boys do) of the English early sixteenth century from a text, then go and live with the Holbeins for a week and see what an enormously greater thing you will possess at the end of it. It is indeed one of the misfortunes of European history that from the fifth century to at least the eleventh we are, so far as Western European history is concerned, deprived of portraits. And by an interesting parallel the writers of the dark time seemed to have had neither the desire nor the gift of vivid description. Consider the dreariness of the hagiographers, every one of them boasting the noble rank and the conventional status of his hero, and you may say not one giving the least conception of the man's personality. You have the great Gallo-Roman noble family of Ferreolus running down the centuries from the Decline of the Empire to the climax of Charlemagne. Many of those names stand for some most powerful individuality, yet all we have is a formula, a lineage, with symbols and names in the place of living beings, and even that established only by careful work, picking out and sifting relationships from various lives. The men of that time did not even think to tell us that there was such a thing as a family tradition, nor did it seem important to them to establish its Roman origin and its long succession in power.

Next it must be protested that the smallness and particularity of the questions upon which historical discussion rages are no proof either of its general purposelessness nor of their insignificance. All advance of knowledge proceeds in this fashion. Physical science affords innumerable examples of the way in which progress has depended upon a curiosity directed towards apparently insignificant things, and there is something in the mind which compels it to select a narrow field for the exercise of its acutest powers. Moreover, special points, discussion upon which must evidently be lengthy and may be indefinite, are peculiarly attractive to just that kind of man who by a love of prolonged research enlarges the bounds of knowledge and at the same time strengthens and improves for his fellows by continual exercise all the instruments of their common trade. Take, for instance, this case of the little Dauphin, Louis XVII. It really does not matter to day whether the boy got away or whether he died in prison. It does not prolong the line of the Capetians--the heir to that is present in the Duke of Orleans. It does not even affect our view of any other considerable part of history--save possibly the policy of Louis XVIII--and it is of no direct interest to our pockets or to our affections. Yet the masses of work which have accumulated round that one doubt have solved twenty other doubts. They have illuminated all the close of the Terror; they are beginning to make us understand that most difficult piece of political psychology, the reaction of Thermidor, and with it how Europeans lose their balance and regain it in the course of their quasi-religious wars; for all our wars have something in them of religion.

Three elements appear to enter into the judgment of history. First, there is the testimony of human witnesses; next, there are the non-human boundaries wherein the action took place, boundaries which, by all our experience, impose fixed limits to action; thirdly, there is that indefinable thing, that mystic power, which all nations deriving from the theology of the Western Church have agreed to call, with the schoolman, common sense; a general appreciation which transcends particular appreciations and which can integrate the differentials of evidence. Of this last it is quite impossible to afford a test or to construct a measure; its presence in an argument is none the less as readily felt as fresh air in a room; without it nothing is convincing however laboured, with it, even though it rely upon slight evidence, one has the feeling of walking on a firm road. But it must be "common sense"--it must be of the sort, that is, which is common to man various and general, and it is in this perhaps that history suffers most from the charlatanism and ritual common to all great matters.

Men will have pomp and mystery surrounding important things, and therefore the historians must, consciously or unconsciously, tend to strut, to quote solemn authorities in support, and to make out the vulgar unworthy of their confidence. Hence, by the way, the plague of footnotes.

These had their origin in two sources: the desire to show that one was honest and to prove it by a reference; the desire to elucidate some point which it was not easy to elucidate in the text itself without making the sentence too elaborate and clumsy. Either use may be seen at its best in Gibbon. With the last generation they have served mainly, and sometimes merely, for ritual adornment and terror, not to make clearer or more honest, but to deceive. Thus Taine in his monstrously false history of the Revolution revels in footnotes; you have but to examine a batch of them with care to turn them completely against his own conclusions--they are only put there as a sort of spiked paling to warn off trespassers. Or, again, M. Thibaut, who writes under the name of "Anatole France," gives footnotes by the score in his romance of Joan of Arc, apparently not even caring to examine whether they so much as refer to his text, let alone support it. They seem to have been done by contract.

Another ailment in this department is the negative one, whereby an historian will leave out some aspect which to him, cramped in a study, seems unimportant, but which any plain man moving in the world would have told him to be the essential aspect of the whole matter. For instance, when Napoleon left Madrid on his forced march to intercept Sir John Moore before that general should have reached Benevente, he thought Moore was at Valladolid, when as a fact he was at Sahagun. In Mr. Oman's history of the Peninsular War the error is put thus: "Napoleon had not the comparatively easy task of cutting the road between Valladolid and Astorga, but the much harder one of intercepting that between Sahagun and Astorga."

Why is this egregious nonsense? The facts are right and so are the dates and the names, yet it makes one blush for Oxford history. Why? Because the all-important element of distance is omitted. The very first question a plain man would ask about the case would be, "What were the distances involved?" The academic historian doesn't know, or, at least, doesn't say; yet without an appreciation of the distances the statement has no value. As a fact the distances were such that in the first case (supposing Moore had been at Valladolid) Napoleon would have had to cover nearly three miles to Moore's one to intercept him--an almost superhuman task. In the second case (Moore being as a fact at Sahagun) he would have had to go over four miles to his opponent's one--an absolutely impossible feat.

To march three miles to the enemy's one is what Mr. Oman calls "a comparatively easy task"; to march four to his one is what Mr. Oman calls a "much harder" task; and to write like that is what an informed critic calls bad history.

The other two factors in an historical judgment can be more easily measured.

The non-human elements which, as I have said, are irremovable (save to miracle), are topography, climate, season, local physical conditions, and so forth. They have two valuable characters in aid of history; the first is that they correct the errors of human memory and support the accuracy of details; the second is that they enable us to complete a picture. We can by their aid "see" the physical framework in which an action took place, and such a landscape helps the judgment of things past as it does of things contemporary. Thus the map, the date, the soil, the contours of Crécy field make the traditional spot at which the King of Bohemia fell doubtful; the same factors make it certain that Drouet did not plunge haphazard through Argonne on the night of June 21, 1791, but that he must have gone by one path--which can be determined.

Or, again, take that prime question, why the Prussians did not charge at Valmy. On their failure to do so all the success of the Revolution turned. A man may read Dumouriez, Kellermann, Pully, Botidoux, Massenback, Goethe--there are fifty eye-witnesses at least whose evidence we can collect, and I defy anyone to decide. (Brunswick himself never knew.) But go to that roll of land between Valmy and the high road; go after three days' rain as the allies did, and you will immediately learn. That field between the heights of "The Moon" and the site of old Valmy mill, which is as hard as a brick in summer (when the experts visit it), is a marsh of the worst under an autumn drizzle; no one could have charged.

As for human testimony, three things appear: first, that the witness is not, as in a law court, circumscribed. His relation may vary infinitely in degree of proximity of time or space to the action, from that of an eye-witness writing within the hour to that of a partisan writing at tenth hand a lifetime after. That question of proximity comes first, from the known action of the human mind whereby it transforms colours and changes remembered things. Next there is the character of the witness for the purposes of his testimony. Historians write, too often, as though virtue--or wealth (with which they often confound it)--were the test. It is not, short of a known motive for lying; a murderer or a thief casually witnessing to a thing with which he is familiar is worth more than the best man witnessing in a matter which he understands ill. It was this error which ruined Croker's essay on Charlotte Robespierre's Memoirs. Croker thought, perhaps wisely, that all radicals were scoundrels; he could not accept her editor's evidence, and (by the way) the view of this amateur collector without a tincture of historical scholarship actually imposed itself on Europe for nearly seventy years!

And the third character in the witness is support: the support upon converging lines of other human testimony, most of it indifferent, some (this is essential) casual and by the way--deprived therefore of motive.

When I shall find these canons satisfied to oppose the strong probability and tradition of the Dauphin's death in prison I shall doubt that death, but not before.

The Absence of the Past

It is perhaps not possible to put into human language that emotion which rises when a man stands upon some plot of European soil and can say with certitude to himself: "Such and such great, or wonderful, or beautiful things happened here."

Touch that emotion ever so lightly and it tumbles into the commonplace, and the deadest of commonplace. Neglect it ever so little and the Present (which is never really there, for even as you walk across Trafalgar Square it is yesterday and tomorrow that are in your mind), the Present, I say, or rather the immediate flow of things, occupies you altogether. But there is a mood, and it is a mood common in men who have read and who have travelled, in which one is overwhelmed by the sanctity of a place on which men have done this or that a long, long time ago.

Here it is that the gentle supports which have been framed for human life by that power which launched it come in and help a man. Time does not remain, but space does, and though we cannot seize the Past physically we can stand physically upon the site, and we can have (if I may so express myself) a physical communion with the Past by occupying that very spot which the past greatness of man or of event has occupied.

It was but the other day that, with an American friend at my side, I stood looking at the little brass plate which says that here Charles Stuart faced (he not only faced, but he refused) the authority of his judges. I know not by what delicate mechanism of the soul that record may seem at one moment a sort of tourist thing, to be neglected or despised, and at another moment a portent. But I will confess that all of a sudden, pointing out this very well-known record upon the brass let into the stone in Westminster Hall, I suddenly felt the presence of the thing. Here all that business was done: they were alive; they were in the Present as we are. Here sat that tender-faced, courageous man, with his pointed beard and his luminous eyes; here he was a living man holding his walking-stick with the great jewel in the handle of it; here was spoken in the very tones of his voice (and how a human voice perishes!--how we forget the accents of the most loved and the most familiar voices within a few days of their disappearance!); here the small gestures, and all the things that make up a personality, marked out Charles Stuart. When the soul is seized with such sudden and positive conviction of the substantial past it is overwhelmed; and Europe is full of such ghosts.

As you take the road to Paradise, about halfway there you come to an inn, which even as inns go is admirable. You go into the garden of it, and see the great trees and the wall of Box Hill shrouding you all around. It is beautiful enough (in all conscience) to arrest one without the need of history or any admixture of the pride of race; but as you sit there on a seat in that garden you are sitting where Nelson sat when he said goodbye to his Emma, and if you will move a yard or two you will be sitting where Keats sat biting his pen and thinking out some new line of his poem.

What has happened? These two men with their keen, feminine faces, these two great heroes of a great time in the great story of a great people of this world, are not there. They are nowhere. But the site remains. Philosophers can put in formulae the crowd of suggestions that rush into the mind when one's soul contemplates the perpetual march and passage of mortality. But they can do no more than give us formularies: they cannot give us replies. What are we? What is all this business? Why does the mere space remain and all the rest dissolve?

There is a lonely place in the woods of Chilham, in the County of Kent, above the River Stour, where a man comes upon an irregular earthwork still plainly marked upon the brow of the bluff. Nobody comes near this place. A vague country lane, or rather track; goes past the wet soil of it, plunges into the valley beyond, and after serving a windmill joins the high road to Canterbury. Well, that vague track is the ancient British road, as old as anything in this Island, that took men from Winchester to the Straits of Dover. That earthwork is the earthwork (I could prove it, but this is not the place) where the British stood against the charge of the Tenth Legion, and first heard, sounding on their bronze, the arms of Caesar. Here the river was forded; here the little men of the South went up in formation; here the Barbarian broke and took his way, as the opposing General has recorded, through devious woodland paths, scattering in the pursuit; here began the great history of England.

Is it not an enormous business merely to stand in such a place? I think so.

I know a field to the left of the Chalons Road, some few miles before you get to Ste. Menehould. There used to be an inn by the roadside called "The Sign of the Moon." It has disappeared. There used to be a ramshackle windmill beyond the field, a mile or so from the road, on an upland swell of land, but that also has gone, and had been gone for some time before I knew the field of which I write. It is a bare fold of land with one or two little scrubby spinneys alongside the plough. And for the rest, just the brown earth and the sky. There are days on which you will see a man at work somewhere within that mile, others on which it is completely deserted. Here it is that the French Revolution was preserved. Here was the Prussian charge. On the deserted, ugly lump of empty earth beyond you were the three batteries that checked the invaders. It was all alive and crowded for one intense moment with the fate of Christendom. Here, on the place in which you are standing and gazing, young Goethe stood and gazed. That meaningless stretch of coarse grass supported Brunswick and the King of Prussia, and the brothers of the King of France, as they stood windswept in the rain, watching the failure of the charge. It is the field of Valmy. Turn on that height and look back westward and you see the plains rolling out infinitely; they are the plains upon which Attila was crushed; but there is no one there.

All men have remarked that night and silence are august, and I think that if this quality in night and silence be closely examined it will be found to consist, in part at least, in this: that either of them symbolizes Absence. By a paradox which I will not attempt to explain, but which all have felt, it is in silence and in darkness that the Past most vividly returns, and that this absence of what once was possesses, nay, obtrudes itself upon the mind: it becomes almost a sensible thing. There is much to be said for those who pretend, imagine, or perhaps have experienced under such conditions the return of the dead. The mood of darkness and of silence is a mood crammed with something that does not remain, as space remains, that is limited by time, and is a creature of time, and yet something that has an immortal right to remain.

Now, I suppose that in that sentence where I say things mortal have immortal rights to permanence, the core of the whole business is touched upon. And I suppose that the great men who could really think and did not merely fire off fireworks to dazzle their contemporaries--I suppose that Descartes, for instance, if he were here sitting at my table--could help me to solve that contradiction; but I sit and think and cannot solve it.

"What," says the man upon his own land, inherited perhaps and certainly intended for his posterity--"what! Can you separate me from this? Are not this and I bound up inextricably?" The answer is "No; you are not so far as any observer of this world can discover. Space is in no way possessed by man, and he who may render a site immortal in one of our various ways, the captain who there conquered, the poet who there established his sequence of words, cannot himself put forward a claim to permanence within it at all."

There was a woman of charming vivacity, whose eyes were

ever ready for laughter, and whose tone of address of itself provoked the noblest of replies. Many loved her; all admired. She passed (I will suppose) by this street or by that; she sat at table in such and such a house; Gainsborough painted her; and all that time ago there were men who had the luck to meet her and to answer her laughter with their own. And the house where she moved is there and the street in which she walked, and the very furniture she used and touched with her hands you may touch with your hands. You shall come into the rooms that she inhabited, and there you shall see her portrait, all light and movement and grace and beatitude.

She is gone altogether, the voice will never return, the gestures will never be seen again. She was under a law; she changed, she suffered, she grew old, she died; and there was her place left empty. The not living things remain; but what counted, what gave rise to them, what made them all that they are, has pitifully disappeared, and the greater, the infinitely greater, thing was subject to a doom perpetually of change and at last of vanishing. The dead surroundings are not subject to such a doom. Why?

All those boys who held the line of the low ridge or rather swell of land from Hougoumont through the Belle Alliance have utterly gone. More than dust goes, more than wind goes; they will never be seen again. Their voices will never be heard--they are not. But what is the mere soil of the field without them? What meaning has it save for their presence?

I could wish to understand these things.

St. Patrick

If there is one thing that people who are not Catholic have gone wrong upon more than another in the intellectual things of life, it is the conception of a Personality. They are muddled about it where their own little selves are concerned, they misappreciate it when they deal with the problems of society, and they have a very weak hold of it when they consider (if they do consider) the nature of Almighty God.

Now, personality is everything. It was a Personal Will that made all things, visible and invisible. Our hope of immortality resides in this, that we are persons, and half our frailties proceed from a misapprehension of the awful responsibilities which personality involves or a cowardly ignorance of its powers of self-government.

The hundred and one errors which this main error leads to include a bad error on the nature of history. Your modern non-Catholic or anti-Catholic historian is always misunderstanding, underestimating, or muddling the role played in the affairs of men by great and individual Personalities. That is why he is so lamentably weak upon the function of legend; that is why he makes a fetish of documentary evidence and has no grip upon the value of tradition. For traditions spring from some personality invariably, and the function of legend, whether it be a rigidly true legend or one tinged with make-believe, is to interpret Personality. Legends have vitality and continue, because in their origin they so exactly serve to explain or illustrate some personal character in a man which no cold statement could give.

Now St. Patrick, the whole story and effect of him, is a matter of Personality. There was once--twenty or thirty years ago--a whole school of dunderheads who wondered whether St. Patrick ever existed, because the mass of legends surrounding his name troubled them. How on earth (one wonders) do such scholars consider their fellow-beings! Have they ever seen a crowd cheering a popular hero, or noticed the expression upon men's faces when they spoke of some friend of striking power recently dead? A great growth of legends around a man is the very best proof you could have not only of his existence but of the fact that he was an origin and a beginning, and that things sprang from his will or his vision. There were some who seemed to think it a kind of favour done to the indestructible body of Irish Catholicism when Mr. Bury wrote his learned Protestant book upon St. Patrick. It was a critical and very careful bit of work, and was deservedly praised; but the favour done us I could not see! It is all to the advantage of non-Catholic history that it should be sane, and that a great Protestant historian should make true history out of a great historical figure was a very good sign. It was a long step back towards common sense compared with the German absurdities which had left their victims doubting almost all the solid foundation of the European story; but as for us Catholics, we had no need to be told it. Not only was there a St. Patrick in history, but there is a St. Patrick on the shores of his eastern sea and throughout all Ireland to-day. It is a presence that stares you in the face, and physically almost haunts you. Let a man sail along the Leinster coast on such a day as renders the Wicklow Mountains clear up-weather behind him, and the Mourne Mountains perhaps in storm, lifted clearly above the sea down the wind. He is taking some such course as that on which St. Patrick sailed, and if he will land from time to time from his little boat at the end of each day's sailing, and hear Mass in the morning before he sails further northward, he will know in what way St. Patrick inhabits the soil which he rendered sacred.

We know that among the marks of holiness is the working of miracles. Ireland is the greatest miracle any saint ever worked. It is a miracle and a nexus of miracles. Among other miracles it is a nation raised from the dead.

The preservation of the Faith by the Irish is an historical miracle comparable to nothing else in Europe. There never was, and please God never can be, so prolonged and insanely violent a persecution of men by their fellow-men as was undertaken for centuries against the Faith in Ireland: and it has completely failed. I know of no example in history of failure following upon such effort. It had behind it in combination the two most powerful of the evil passions of men, terror and greed. And so amazing is it that they did not attain their end, that perpetually as one reads one finds the authors of the dreadful business now at one period, now at another, assuming with certitude that their success is achieved. Then, after centuries, it is almost suddenly perceived--and in our own time--that it has not been achieved and never will be.

What a complexity of strange coincidences combined, coming out of nothing as it were, advancing like spirits summoned on to the stage, all to effect this end! Think of the American Colonies; with one little exception they were perhaps the most completely non-Catholic society of their time. Their successful rebellion against the mother country meant many things, and led to many prophecies. Who could have guessed that one of its chief results would be the furnishing of a free refuge for the Irish?

The famine, all human opinion imagined, and all human judgment was bound to conclude, was a mortal wound, coming in as the ally of the vile persecution I have named. It has turned out the very contrary. From it there springs indirectly the dispersion, and that power which comes from unity in dispersion, of Irish Catholicism.

Who, looking at the huge financial power that dominated Europe, and England in particular, during the youth of our own generation, could have dreamt that in any corner of Europe, least of all in the poorest and most ruined corner of Christendom, an effective resistance could be raised?

Behind the enemies of Ireland, furnishing them with all their modern strength, was that base and secret master of modern things, the usurer. He it was far more than the gentry of the island who demanded toll, and, through the mortgages on the Irish estates, had determined to drain Ireland as he has drained and rendered desert so much else. Is it not a miracle that he has failed?

Ireland is a nation risen from the dead; and to raise one man from the dead is surely miraculous enough to convince one of the power of a great spirit. This miracle, as I am prepared to believe, is the last and the greatest of St. Patrick's.

When I was last in Ireland, I bought in the town of Wexford a coloured picture of St. Patrick which greatly pleased me. Most of it was green in colour, and St. Patrick wore a mitre and had a crosier in his hand. He was turning into the sea a number of nasty reptiles: snakes and toads and the rest. I bought this picture because it seemed to me as modern a piece of symbolism as ever I had seen: and that was why I bought it for my children and for my home.

There was a few pence change, but I did not want it. The person who sold me the picture said they would spend the change in candles for St. Patrick's altar. So St. Patrick is still alive.

The Lost Things

I never remember an historian yet, nor a topographer either, who could tell me, or even pretend to explain by a theory, how it was that certain things of the past utterly and entirely disappear.

It is a commonplace that everything is subject to decay, and a commonplace which the false philosophy of our time is too apt to forget. Did we remember that commonplace we should be a little more humble in our guesswork, especially where it concerns prehistory; and we should not make so readily certain where the civilization of Europe began, nor limit its immense antiquity. But though it is a commonplace, and a true one, that all human work is subject to decay, there seems to be an inexplicable caprice in the method and choice of decay.

Consider what a body of written matter there must have been to instruct and maintain the technical excellence of Roman work. What a mass of books on engineering and on ship-building and on road-making; what quantities of tables and ready-reckoners, all that civilization must have produced and depended upon. Time has preserved much verse, and not only the best by any means, more prose, particularly the theological prose of the end of the Roman time. The technical stuff, which must, in the nature of things, have been indefinitely larger in amount, has (save in one or two instances and allusions) gone.

Consider, again, all that mass of seven hundred years which was called Carthage. It was not only seven hundred years of immense wealth, of oligarchic government, of a vast population, and of what so often goes with commerce and oligarchy--civil and internal peace. A few stones to prove the magnitude of its municipal work, a few ornaments, a few graves--all the rest is absolutely gone. A few days' marches away there is an example I have quoted so often elsewhere that I am ashamed of referring to it again, but it does seem to me the most amazing example of historical loss in the world. It is the site of Hippo Regius. Here was St. Augustine's town, one of the greatest and most populous of a Roman province. It was so large that an army of eighty thousand men could not contain it, and even with such a host its siege dragged on for a year. There is not a sign of that great town today.

A suburb, well without the walls--to be more accurate, a neighbouring village--carries on the name under the form of Bona, and that is all. A vast, fertile plain of black rich earth, now largely planted with vineyards, stands where Hippo stood. How can the stones have gone? How can it have been worth while to cart away the marble columns? Why are there no broken statues on such a ground, and no relics of the gods?

Nay, the wells are stopped up from which the people drank, and the lining of the wells is not to be discovered in the earth, and the foundations of the walls, and even the ornaments of the people and their coins, all these have been spirited away.

Then there are the roads. Consider that great road which reached from Amiens to the main port of Gaul, the Portus Itius at Boulogne. It is still in use. It was in use throughout the Middle Ages. Up that road the French Army marched to Crécy. It points straight to its goal upon the sea coast. Its whole purpose lay in reaching the goal. For some extraordinary reason, which I have never seen explained or even guessed at, there comes a point as it nears the coast where it suddenly ceases to be.

No sand has blown over it. It runs through no marshes; the land is firm and fertile. Why should that, the most important section of the great road which led northward from Rome, have failed, and have failed so recently, in the history of man? Where this great road crosses streams and might reasonably be lost, at its pontes, its bridges, it has remained, and is of such importance as to have given a name to a whole countryside--Ponthieu. But north of that it is gone.

Nearly every Roman road of Gaul and Britain presents something of the same puzzle in some parts of its course. It will run clear and followable enough, or form a modern highway for mile upon mile, and then not at a marsh where one would expect its disappearance, nor in some desolate place where it might have fallen out of use, but in the neighbourhood of a great city and at the very chief of its purpose, it is gone. It is so with the Stane Street that led up from the garrison of Chichester and linked it with the garrison of London. You can reconstruct it almost to a yard until you reach Epsom Downs. There you find it pointing to London Bridge, and remaining as clear as in any other part of its course: much clearer than in most other sections. But try to follow it on from Epsom Racecourse, and you entirely fail. The soil is the same; the conditions of that soil are excellent for its retention; but a year's work has taught me that there is no reconstructing it save by hypothesis and guesswork from this point to the crossing of the Thames.

What happened to all that mass of local documents whereby we ought to be able to build up the territorial scheme and the landed regime of old France? Much remains, if you will, in the shape of chance charters and family papers. Even in the archives of

51

Paris you can get enough to whet your curiosity. But not even in one narrow district can you obtain enough to reconstruct the whole truth. There is not a scholar in Europe who can tell you exactly how land was owned and held, even, let us say, on the estates of Rheims or by the family of Condé. And men are ready to quarrel as to how many peasants owned and how much of their present ownership was due to the Revolution, evidence has already become so wholly imperfect in that tiny stretch of historical time.

But, after all, perhaps one ought not to wonder too much that material things should thus capriciously vanish. Time, which has secured Timgad so that it looks like an unroofed city of yesterday, has swept and razed Laimboesis. The two towns were neighbours-- one was taken and the other left--and there is no sort of reason any man can give for it. Perhaps one ought not too much to wonder, for a greater wonder still is the sudden evaporation and loss of the great movements of the human soul. That what our ancestors passionately believed or passionately disputed should, by their descendants in one generation or in two, become meaningless, absurd, or false--this is the greatest marvel and the greatest tragedy of all.

On the Reading of History

Let me at the beginning of this short article present two facts to the reader. Neither can be disputed, and that is why I call them facts and put them in the forefront before I begin upon my theories.

The first fact is that the record of what men have done in the past and how they have done it is the chief positive guide to present action. The second fact is that most men must now receive the impression of the past through reading.

Put these two facts together and you get the fundamental truth that upon the right reading of history the right use of citizenship in England today will depend. It will of course depend upon other things as well: chiefly upon the human conscience; for if you were to pack off to an island a hundred families as ignorant as any human families can be of tradition, and wholly ignorant of positive history, those families would yet be able to create a human society and the voice of God within them would give just limits to their actions.

Still, of those factors in civic action amenable to civic direction, conscious and positively effective, there is nothing to compare with the right teaching and the right reading of history. Now teaching is today ruined. The old machinery by which the whole nation could be got to know all essential human things, has been destroyed, and the teaching of history in particular has been not only ruined but rendered ridiculous. There is no historical school properly so-called in modern England; that is, there is no organization framed with the sole object of extending and co-ordinating historical knowledge and of choosing men for their capacity to discover upon the one hand and to teach upon the other. There is nothing approaching to it in the two ancient universities, because the choice of teachers there depends upon a multitude of considerations quite separate from those mentioned, and the capacity to discover, to know, and to teach history, though it may be present in a tutor, will only be accidentally so present: while as for co-ordination of knowledge, there is no attempt at it. Even where very hard work is done, and, when it concerns local history, very useful work, history as a general study is not grasped because the universities have not grasped it.

History is to be had by the modern Englishman from his own reading only; and I am here concerned with the question how he shall read history with profit.

To read history with profit, history must be true, or at any rate the reader must have a power of discerning what is true in the midst of much that may be false. I will bargain, for instance, that in the summer of 1899 the great mass of men, and especially the great mass of men who had passed through the universities, were under the impression that armies had left England for the purpose of conquest in distant countries with invariable success: that that success had been unique, unsupported and always decisive, and that the wealth of the country after each success had increased, not diminished. In other words, had history been studied even by the tiny minority who have education today in England, Sir William Butler would have counted more than the Joels, and the late Mr. Barnato (as he called himself); the South African War would not have taken place in a society which knew its past.

Again, you may pick almost any phrase referring to the Middle Ages out of any newspaper--if you are a man read in the Middle Ages--and you will find in it not only a definite historical falsehood with regard to the fact referred to, or the analogy drawn, but also a false philosophy.

For instance, the other day I read this phrase with regard to the burial of a certain gentleman of my neighbourhood in Sussex: "We are surely past the phase of mediaeval thought in which it was imagined that a few words spoken over the lifeless clay would determine the fate of the soul for all eternity." Just notice the myriad falsehoods of a phrase like that! I will not discuss what is connoted by the words "past the phase of mediaeval thought"--it connotes of course that the human mind changes fundamentally with the centuries, and therefore that whatever we think is probably wrong, and that what we are sure of we cannot be sure of, an absurd conclusion. I will only note the historical falsehoods. When on earth did the "Middle Ages" lay down that a "few words over lifeless clay determined the fate of the soul for all eternity"? On the contrary, the Middle Ages laid it down--it was their peculiar doctrine--that it was impossible to determine the fate of the soul; that no one could tell the fate of any one individual soul; that it was a grievous sin, among the most grievous of sins, to affirm positive knowledge that any individual had lost his soul. More than this, the Middle Ages were peculiar in their insistence upon the doctrine that a man might have been very bad and might have had all the appearance of having lost his soul so far as human judgment went, and yet was liable to a midway place between salvation and damnation, and they affirmed that this midway place did not lead to either fate but necessarily to salvation and to salvation only.

Again, whatever could help the human soul to salvation was by the most rigorous theological definition of the Middle Ages applicable only before death. After death the fate of the soul was sealed, and the man once dead, the "lifeless clay" (as the journalist put it--and the Middle Ages was the only source from which he got the idea of clay at all), whether it were that of a Pope or of some random highwayman, had no effect whatsoever upon the fate of the soul. The greatest saint might have offered the most solemn sacrifice on its behalf for years, and if the soul were damned his sacrifice would have been of no avail.

I have taken this example absolutely at random. But the modern reader, apart from sentences as clearly provocative of criticism as this, is perpetually coming across references, allusions, and parallels which take a certain course of human European and English history for granted. How is he to distinguish when that course is rightly drawn from when it is wrongly drawn?

Thus in some newspaper article written by an able man, and dealing, let us say, with the territorial army, one might come across a sentence like this: "Napoleon himself used troops so raw that they were actually drilled on the march to the battlefield." That would be a perfectly true statement. Any amount of criticism of it lies in connexion with Mr. Haldane's scheme, but still it is a true piece of history. Napoleon did get raw recruits into his battalions just before any one of his famous marches began, and drill them on the way to victory. In the next column of the newspaper the reader may be presented with a sentence like this: "The captures of English by privateers in the Revolutionary War should teach us what foreign cruisers can do."

There were plenty of captures by privateers in the Revolutionary Wars; if I remember rightly, many many hundreds, all discreetly hidden from the common or garden reader until party politics necessitated their resurrection a hundred years after the event, but they have nothing whatsoever to do with modern circumstances.

Both statements are true then, and yet one can be truthfully applied today, while the other cannot.

How is the plain reader to distinguish between two historical truths, one of which is a useful modern analogy, the other of which is a ludicrously misleading one?

The reader, it would seem, has no criterion by which to distinguish what has been withheld from him and what has been emphasized; he may, from his knowledge of the historian's character or bias, stand upon his guard, but he can do little more.

There is another difficulty. It is less subtle and less common, but it exists. I mean brute lying. You do not often get the lie direct in official history; it would be too dangerous a game to play in the face of the critics, though some historians, and notably the French historian Taine, have played it boldly enough, and have stated dogmatically, as historical happenings, things that never happened and that they knew never happened. But the plain or brute historical lie is more commonly found in the pages of ephemeral journalism. Thus the other day, with regard to the Budget, I saw some financial operation alluded to as comparable with "the pulling out of Jews' teeth for money in the Middle Ages." When did anyone in the Middle Ages pull out a Jew's teeth for money? There is just one very doubtful story told about King John, and that story is told without proof by one of John's worst enemies, in a mass of other accusations many of which can be proved to be false.

Again, I turn to an Oxford History of the French Revolution, and I find the remark that the massacres of September were organized by the men from Marseilles. They were not organized by the men from Marseilles. The men from Marseilles had nothing to do with them, and the fact has been public property since the publication of Pollio and Marcel's monograph twenty years ago.

What criterion can the ordinary reader choose when he is confronted by difficulties of this sort? I will suggest to him one which seems to me by far the most valuable. It is the reading of firsthand authorities. It is all a matter of habit. When the original authorities upon which history is based were difficult to get at, when few of those in foreign tongues had been translated, and when those that had been published were published in the most expensive form, the ordinary reader had to depend upon an historian who would summarize for him the reading of another. The ordinary reader was compelled to read secondary history or none. Now secondary history is among the most valuable of literary efforts; where evidence is slight, the judgment of an historian who knows from other reading the general character of the period, is most valuable. Where evidence is abundant, and therefore confusing, the historian used to the selection and weighing of it performs a most valuable function. Still, the reader who is not acquainted with original authorities does not really know history and is at the mercy of whatever myth or tradition may be handed to him in print.

We should remember that today, even in England, original authorities are quite easy to get at. Two little books, for instance, occur to me out of hundreds: Mr. Rait's book on Mary Stuart and Mr. Archer's on the Third Crusade. In each of these the reader gets in a cheap form, in modern and readable English, the kind of evidence upon which historians base their history, and he can use that evidence in the light of his own knowledge of human nature and his own judgment of human life.

Or again, if he wants to know what the Romans really knew or said they knew about the German tribes who, as pirates, so greatly influenced the history of England, let him get Mr. Rouse's edition of Grenewey's translation of the Germania in Blackie's series of English texts; it will only cost sixpence, and for that money he will get a bit of Caesar's Gallic War and the Agricola as well. But the list nowadays is a very long one, luckily, and the lay reader has only to choose what period he would like to read up, and he will find for nearly every one first-hand evidence ready, cheap and published in a readable modern form. That he should take such first-hand evidence is the very best advice that any honest historian can give.

The Victory

The study of history, like the exploration, the thorough exploration, of any other field, leads one to perpetual novelties, miracles, and unexpected things; and I, in the study of the revolutionary wars, came across the story of a battle which completely possessed my spirit.

It would not be to my purpose here to give its name. It is not among the most famous; it is not Waterloo, nor Leipsic, nor Austerlitz, nor even Jemappes. The more I read into the night the more I perceived that upon the issue of that struggle depended the fate of the modern world. So completely did the notes of Carnot and a few private letters that had been put before me absorb my attention that I will swear the bugle-calls of those two days (for it was a two-days' struggle) sounded more clearly in my ears than the rumble of the London streets, and, as this died out with the advance of the night and the approach of morning, I was living entirely upon that ridge in Flanders, watching, as a man watches an arena, whether the new things or the old should be victorious. It was the new that conquered.

From that evening I was determined to visit this place of which so far I had but read, and to see how far it might agree with the vision I had had of it, and to people actual fields with the ghosts of dead soldiers. And for the better appreciation of the drama I chose the season and the days on which the fight had been driven across that rolling land, and I came there, as the Republicans had come, a little before the dawn.

The hillside was silent and deserted, more even than are commonly such places, though silence and desertion seem the common atmosphere of all the fields on which such fates have been decided. A man looking over Carthage Bay, especially a man looking at those sodden pools that were the sound harbours of Carthage, might be in an uninhabited world; and the loop of the Trebbia is the same, and the edge of Fontenoy; and even here in England that hillside looking south up which the Normans charged at Battle is a quiet and a drowsy sort of place.... So it was here in Flanders.

For two miles as I ascended by the little sunken lane which the extreme right wing had followed in the last attack I saw neither man nor beast, but only the same stubble of the same autumn fields, and the same colder sun shining upon the empty uplands until I reached the crest where the Hungarian and the Croat had met the charge, and had disputed the little village for two hours--a dispute upon which hung your fate and mine and that of Europe.

It was a tiny little village, seven or eight houses together and no more, with a crazy little wooden steeple to its church all twisted awry, large barns, and comfortable hedgerows of the Northern kind; and from it one looked out westwards over an infinity of country, following low crest after low crest, down on to the French plains. I went into the inn of the place to drink, and found the cobbler there complaining that wealth disturbed the natural equality of men. Then I wandered out, pacing this point and that which I knew accurately from my maps, and thinking of the noise of the war. Behind the little church, upon a ramshackle green not large enough to pitch the stumps for single-wicket, was the modest monument, a cock in bronze, crowing, and the word "Victory" stamped into the granite of the pedestal; the whole thing, I suppose, not ten feet high. The bronze was very well done; it savoured strongly of Paris and looked odd in this abandoned little place. But every time my eyes sank from the bronze, to look at some other point in the landscape to identify the emplacement of such and such a battery or the gully that had concealed the advance of such and such a troop, my glance perpetually returned to that word "VICTORY," sculptured by itself upon the stone. It was indeed a victory; it was a victory which, for its huge unexpectedness, for the noise of it, for the length of time during which it was in doubt, for its final success, there is no parallel, and yet it is by no means among the famous battles of the world. And though the French count it one among the thousand of their battles, I doubt whether even in Paris most men would recognize it for the hammer-blow it was. The men of the time hardly knew it, though Carnot guessed at it, and now to-day in Sorbonne I think that regal fight is taking its true place.

So I went down the eight miles of front northward along the ridge; for even that battle, a hundred and more years ago, had an extended front of this kind. I recognized the tall majestic fringe of beeches from which had issued the last of the Royalist regiments bearing for the last time upon a European field the white flag of the Bourbon Monarchy; I came beyond it to the combe fringed with its semicircle of underbrush in which Coburg had massed his guns in the last effort to break the French centre when his flank was turned. I came to the main highway, very broad, straight, and paved, which cuts this battlefield in two, and then beyond it to the central position whose capture had made the final manoeuvre possible.

All Wednesday the Grenadiers, German, tall, padded, smart, and stout, had held their ground. It was not until Thursday, and by noon, that they were slowly driven up the hill by the ragged lads, the Gauls, shoeless, some not in uniform at all, half-mutinous, drunk with pain and glory. And I remembered, as the scene returned to

59

me, that this battle, like so many of the Revolution, had been a battle of men against boys; how grey and veteran and trained in arms were the Austrians and the Prussians, their allies, how strict in orders, how calm: and what children the Terror had called up by force from the exhausted fields of remote French provinces, to break them here against the frontier, like water against a wall...!

There was a little chap, twelve years old, a drummer; he had crept and crawled by hedgerows till he found himself behind the line of those volleying Grenadiers. There, "before his side," and breaking all rules, he had sounded the roll of the charge. They cut him down and killed him, and the roll of his drum ceased hard. A generation or more later, digging for foundations at this spot, the builders of the Peace came upon his bones, the little bones of a child heaped pell-mell with skeletons of the fallen giants round him.

I went back into the town in whose defence the battle had been waged, and there I saw again in bronze this little lad, head high and mouth open, a-beating of his drum, and again the word "VICTORY."

All that effort was undertaken, all those young men and children killed, for something that was to happen for the salvation of the world; it has not come. All that iron resistance of the German line had been forged and organized till it almost conquered, till it almost thwarted, the Republic, and it also had been organized for the defence, and, as some thought, for the salvation, of the world. Some great good was to have come by the storming of that hill, or some great good by the defeat of the impetuous charge. Well, the hill was stormed, and (if you will) at Leipsic the effort which had stormed it was rolled back. What has happened to the High Goddess whom that youth followed, and worshipped as they say, and what to the Gods whom their enemies defended? The ridge is exactly the same.

Reality

A couple of generations ago there was a sort of man going mournfully about who complained of the spread of education. He had an ill-ease in his mind. He feared that book learning would bring us no good, and he was called a fool for his pains. Not undeservedly--for his thoughts were muddled, and if his heart was good it was far better than his head. He argued badly or he merely affirmed, but he had strong allies (Ruskin was one of them), and, like every man who is sincere, there was something in what he said; like every type which is numerous, there was a human feeling behind him: and he was very numerous.

Now that he is pretty well extinct we are beginning to understand what he meant and what there was to be said for him. The greatest of the French Revolutionists was right--"After bread, the most crying need of the populace is knowledge." But what knowledge?

The truth is that secondary impressions, impressions gathered from books and from maps, are valuable as adjuncts to primary impressions (that is, impressions gathered through the channel of our senses), or, what is always almost as good and sometimes better, the interpreting voice of the living man. For you must allow me the paradox that in some mysterious way the voice and gesture of a living witness always convey something of the real impression he has had, and sometimes convey more than we should have received ourselves from our own sight and hearing of the thing related.

Well, I say, these secondary impressions are valuable as adjuncts to primary impressions. But when they stand absolute and have hardly any reference to primary impressions, then they may deceive. When they stand not only absolute but clothed with authority, and when they pretend to convince us even against our own experience, they are positively undoing the work which education was meant to do. When we receive them merely as an enlargement of what we know and make of the unseen things of which we read, things in the image of the seen, then they quite distort our appreciation of the world.

Consider so simple a thing as a river. A child learns its map and knows, or thinks it knows, that such and such rivers characterize such and such nations and their territories. Paris stands upon the River Seine, Rome upon the River Tiber, New Orleans on the Mississippi, Toledo upon the River Tagus, and so forth. That child will know one river, the river near his home. And he will think of all those other rivers in its image. He will think of the Tagus and the Tiber and the Seine and the Mississippi--and they will all be the river near his home. Then let him travel, and what will he come across? The Seine, if he is from these islands, may not disappoint him or astonish him with a sense of novelty and of ignorance. It will indeed look grander and more majestic, seen from the enormous forest heights above its lower course, than what, perhaps, he had thought possible in a river, but still it will be a river of water out of which a man can drink, with clear-cut banks and with bridges over it, and with boats that ply up and down. But let him see the Tagus at Toledo, and what he finds is brown rolling mud, pouring solid after the rains, or sluggish and hardly a river after long drought. Let him go down the Tiber, down the Valley of the Tiber, on foot, and he will retain until the last miles an impression of nothing but a turbid mountain torrent, mixed with the friable soil in its bed. Let him approach the Mississippi in the most part of its long course and the novelty will be more striking still. It will not seem to him a river at all (if he be from Northern Europe); it will seem a chance flood. He will come to it through marshes and through swamps, crossing a deserted backwater, finding firm land beyond, then coming to further shallow patches of wet, out of which the tree-stumps stand, and beyond which again mud-heaps and banks and groups of reeds leave undetermined, for one hundred yards after another, the limits of the vast stream. At last, if he has a boat with him, he may make some place where he has a clear view right across to low trees, tiny from their distance, similarly half swamped upon a further shore, and behind them a low escarpment of bare earth. That is the Mississippi nine times out of ten, and to an Englishman who had expected to find from his early reading or his maps a larger Thames it seems for all the world like a stretch of East Anglian flood, save that it is so much more desolate.

The maps are coloured to express the claims of Governments. What do they tell you of the social truth? Go on foot or bicycling through the more populated upland belt of Algiers and discover the curious mixture of security and war which no map can tell you of and which none of the geographies make you understand. The excellent roads, trodden by men that cannot make a road; the walls as ready loopholed for fighting; the Christian church and the mosque in one town; the necessity for and the hatred of the European; the indescribable difference of the sun, which here, even in winter, has something malignant about it, and strikes as well as

62

warms; the mountains odd, unlike our mountains; the forests, which stand as it were by hardihood, and seem at war against the influence of dryness and the desert winds, with their trees far apart, and between them no grass, but bare earth alone.

So it is with the reality of arms and with the reality of the sea. Too much reading of battles has ever unfitted men for war; too much talk of the sea is a poison in these great town populations of ours which know nothing of the sea. Who that knows anything of the sea will claim certitude in connexion with it? And yet there is a school which has by this time turned its mechanical system almost into a commonplace upon our lips, and talks of that most perilous thing, the fortunes of a fleet, as though it were a merely numerical and calculable thing! The greatest of Armadas may set out and not return.

There is one experience of travel and of the physical realities of the world which has been so widely repeated, and which men have so constantly verified, that I could mention it as a last example of my thesis without fear of misunderstanding. I mean the quality of a great mountain.

To one that has never seen a mountain it may seem a full and a fine piece of knowledge to be acquainted with its height in feet exactly, its situation; nay, many would think themselves learned if they know no more than its conventional name. But the thing itself! The curious sense of its isolation from the common world, of its being the habitation of awe, perhaps the brooding-place of a god!

I had seen many mountains, I had travelled in many places, and I had read many particular details in the books--and so well noted them upon the maps that I could have re-drawn the maps--concerning the Cerdagne. None the less the sight of that wall of the Cerdagne, when first it struck me, coming down the pass from Tourcarol, was as novel as though all my life had been spent upon empty plains. By the map it was 9000 feet. It might have been 90,000! The wonderment as to what lay beyond, the sense that it was a limit to known things, its savage intangibility, its sheer silence! Nothing but the eye seeing could give one all those things.

The old complain that the young will not take advice. But the wisest will tell them that, save blindly and upon authority, the young cannot take it. For most of human and social experience is words to the young, and the reality can come only with years. The wise complain of the jingo in every country; and properly, for he upsets the plans of statesmen, miscalculates the value of national forces, and may, if he is powerful enough, destroy the true spirit of armies. But the wise would be wiser still if, while they blamed the extravagance of this sort of man, they would recognize that it came from that half-knowledge of mere names and lists which excludes reality. It is maps and newspapers that turn an honest fool into a jingo.

It is so again with distance, and it is so with time. Men will not grasp distance unless they have traversed it, or unless it be represented to them vividly by the comparison of great landscapes. Men will not grasp historical time unless the historian shall be at the pains to give them what historians so rarely give, the measure of a period in terms of a human life. It is from secondary impressions divorced from reality that a contempt for the past arises, and that the fatal illusion of some gradual process of betterment of "progress" vulgarizes the minds of men and wastes their effort. It is from secondary impressions divorced from reality that a society imagines itself diseased when it is healthy, or healthy when it is diseased. And it is from secondary impressions divorced from reality that springs the amazing power of the little second-rate public man in those modern machines that think themselves democracies. This last is a power which, luckily, cannot be greatly abused, for the men upon whom it is thrust are not capable even of abuse upon a great scale. It is none the less marvellous in its falsehood.

Now you will say at the end of this, Since you blame so much the power for distortion and for ill residing in our great towns, in our system of primary education and in our papers and in our books, what remedy can you propose? Why, none, either immediate or mechanical. The best and the greatest remedy is a true philosophy, which shall lead men always to ask themselves what they really know and in what order of certitude they know it; where authority actually resides and where it is usurped. But, apart from the advent, or rather the recapture, of a true philosophy by a European society, two forces are at work which will always bring reality back, though less swiftly and less whole. The first is the poet, and the second is Time.

Sooner or later Time brings the empty phrase and the false conclusion up against what is; the empty imaginary looks reality in the face and the truth at once conquers. In war a nation learns whether it is strong or no, and how it is strong and how weak; it learns it as well in defeat as in victory. In the long processes of human lives, in the succession of generations, the real necessities and nature of a human society destroy any false formula upon which it was attempted to conduct it. Time must always ultimately teach.

The poet, in some way it is difficult to understand (unless we admit that he is a seer), is also very powerful as the ally of such an influence. He brings out the inner part of things and presents them to men in such a way that they cannot refuse but must accept it. But how the mere choice and rhythm of words should produce so magical an effect no one has yet been able to comprehend, and least of all the poets themselves.

On the Decline of the Book

[And Especially of the Historical Book]

It is an interesting speculation by what means the Book lost its old position in this country. This is not only an interesting speculation, but one which nearly concerns a vital matter. For if men fall into the habit of neglecting true books in an old and traditional civilization, the inaccuracy of their judgments and the illusions to which they will be subject, must increase.

To take but one example: history. The less the true historical book is read and the more men depend upon ephemeral statement, the more will legend crystallize, the harder will it be to destroy in the general mind some comforting lie, and the great object-lesson of politics (which is an accurate knowledge of how men have acted in the past) will become at last unknown.

There are many, especially among younger men, who would contest the premiss upon which all this is founded. They may point out, for instance, that the actual number of bound books bought in a given time at present is much larger than ever it was before. They may point out again, and with justice, that the proportion of the population which reads books of any sort, though perhaps not larger than it was three hundred years ago, is very much larger than it was one hundred years ago. And it may further be affirmed with truth that the range of subjects now covered by books produced and sold is much wider than ever it was before.

All this is true; and yet it is also true that the Book as a factor in our civilization has not only declined but has almost disappeared. Were many more dogs to be possessed in England than are now possessed, but were they to be all mongrels, among which none could be found capable of retrieving, or of following a fox or a hare with any discipline, one would have a right to say that the dog as a factor of our civilization had declined. Were many more men in England able to ride horses more or less, but were the number of those who rode constantly and for pleasure enormously to diminish, and were the new millions who could just manage to keep on horseback to prefer animals without spirit on which they would feel safe, one would have a right to say that the horse was declining as a factor in our civilization; and this is exactly what has happened with the Book.

The excellence of a book and its value as a book depend upon two factors, which are usually, though not always, united in varied

66

proportions: first, that it should put something of value to the reader, whether of value as a discovery and an enlargement of wisdom or of value as a new emphasis laid upon old and sound morals; secondly, that this thing added or renewed in human life should be presented in such a manner as to give permanent aesthetic pleasure.

That is not a first-rate book which, while it is admirably written, teaches something false or something evil; nor is that a first-rate book which, though it discover a completely new thing, or emphasize the most valuable department of morals, is so constructed as to be unreadable. Now it will not be denied that as far as these two factors are concerned--and I repeat they are almost always found in combination--the position of the Book has dwindled almost to nothingness. One could give examples of almost every kind: one could show how poetry, no matter how appreciated or praised, no longer sells. One could show--and this is one of the worst signs of all--how men will buy by the hundred thousand anything at all which has the hall mark of an established reputation, quite careless as to their love of it or their appetite for it. One could further show how more than one book of permanent value in English life has been discovered in our generation outside England, and has been as it were thrust upon the English public by foreign opinion.

But for my purpose it will be sufficient to take one very important branch which I can claim to have watched with some care, and that is the branch of History.

It may be said with truth that in our generation no single first-rate piece of history has enjoyed an appreciable sale. That is not true of France, it is not true of the United States, it is not even true of Germany in her intellectual decline, but it is true of England.

History is an excellent test. No man will read history, at least history of an instructive sort, unless he is a man who can read a book, and desires to possess one. To read History involves not only some permanent interest in things not immediately sensible, but also some permanent brain-work in the reader; for as one reads history one cannot, if one is an intelligent being, forbear perpetually to contrast the lessons it teaches with the received opinions of our time. Again, History is valuable as an example in the general thesis I am maintaining, because no good history can be written without a great measure of hard work. To make a history at once accurate, readable, useful, and new, is probably the hardest of all literary efforts; a man writing such history is driving more horses abreast in his team than a man writing any other kind of literary matter. He must keep his imagination active; his style must be not only lucid, but also must arrest the reader; he must exercise perpetually a power of selection which plays over innumerable details; he must, in the midst of such occupations, preserve unity of design, as much as must the novelist or the playwright; and yet with all this there is not a verb, an adjective or a substantive which, if it does not repose upon established evidence, will not mar the particular type of work on which he is engaged.

As an example of what I mean, consider two sentences: The first is taken from the 432nd page of that exceedingly unequal publication, the Cambridge History of the French Revolution; the second I have made up on the spur of the moment; both deal with the Battle of Wattignies. The "Cambridge History" version runs as follows:--

On October 15 the relieving force, 50,000 strong, attacked the Austrian covering force at Wattignies; the battle raged all that day and was most furious on the right, in front of the village of Wattignies, which was taken and lost three times; on the 17th the French expected another general engagement but the enemy had drawn off.

There are here five great positive errors in six lines. The French were not 50,000 strong, the attack on the 15th was not on Wattignies, but on Dourlers; Wattignies was not taken and lost three times; the fight of the 15th was least pressed on the right (harder on the left and hardest in the centre) and no one--not the least recruit--expected Coburg to come back on the 17th. Why, he had crossed the Sambre at every point the day before! As for negative errors, or errors of omission, they are capital, and the chief is that the victory was won on the second day, the 16th, of which no mention is made.

Now contrast such a sentence with the following:--

On October 15th the relieving force, 42,000 strong, attacked the Austrian centre at Dourlers, and made demonstrations upon its wings; the attack upon Dourlers (which village had been taken and lost three times) having failed, upon the following day, October 16th, the extreme left of the enemy's position at Wattignies was attacked and carried; the enemy thus outflanked was compelled to retreat, and Maubeuge was relieved the same evening.

In the first sentence (which bears the hall mark of the University) every error that could possibly be made in so few lines has been made. The numbers are wrong; the nature of the fighting is misstated; the village in the centre is confused with that on the extreme right; the critical second day is altogether omitted, and every portion of the sentence, verb, adjective, and substantive, is either directly inaccurate or indirectly conveys an inaccurate impression. The second sentence, bald in style and uninteresting in presentation as the first, has the merit of telling the truth. But--and here is the point--it would be impossible to criticize the first sentence unless someone had read up the battle, and to read up that battle one has to depend on five or six documents, some unpublished (like much of Jourdan's Memoirs), some of them involving a visit to Maubeuge itself, some, like Pierrat's book, very difficult to obtain (for it is neither in the British Museum nor in the Bodleian) some few the writings of contemporary eyewitnesses, and yet themselves demonstrably inaccurate. All these must be read and collated, and if possible the actual ground of the battle visited, before the first simple inaccurate sentence can be properly criticized or the second bald but accurate sentence framed. None of these authorities can have been so much as heard of by the official historian I have quoted.

It would be redundant to press the point. Most readers know well enough what labour the just writing of history involves, and how excellent a type it is of that "making of a book" which art is, as I have said, imperilled by apathy at the present day.

Consider for a moment who were those that purchased historical works in this country in the past. There were, first of all, the landed gentry. In almost every great country-house you will find a good old library, and that good old library you will discover to be, as a rule, most valuable and most complete in what concerns the end of the eighteenth and the beginning of the nineteenth centuries. A very large proportion of history, and history of the best sort, is to be found upon those shelves. The standard dwindles, though it is fairly well maintained during the first two-thirds of the nineteenth century. Then--as a rule--it abruptly comes to an end. One may take as a sort of bourne, the two great books Macaulay's History and Kinglake's, for an earlier and a later limit. Most of these libraries contain Macaulay; some few Kinglake; hardly one possesses later works of value.

It may be urged in defence of the buyer that no later works of value exist. Put so broadly, the statement is erroneous; but the truth which it contains is in itself dependent upon the lack of public support for good historical work. When there is a fortune for the man who writes in accordance with whatever form of self-appreciation happens for the moment to be popular, while a steady view and an accurate presentation of the past can find no sale, then that steady view and that accurate presentation cannot be pursued save by men who are wealthy, or by men who are endowed, but even wealthy men will hesitate to write what they know will not be read, and for history no one is endowed.

Our Universities were framed for many purposes, of which the cultivation of learning was but one; in that one field, however, a particular form of learning was taken very seriously, and was pursued with admirable industry; I mean an acquaintance with and an imitation of the Latin and Greek Classics.

It was a particular character of this form of learning that proficiency in it would lead to undisputed honours. The scholar recognized the superior scholar; the field of inquiry was by convention highly limited; it had been thoroughly explored; discussion upon such results as were doubtful did not involve a difference in general philosophy.

With history it is otherwise. Whether such things have or have not happened, and, above all, if they have happened, the way in which they have happened, is to our general judgment of contemporary men what evidence is to a criminal trial. Facts won't give way. If, therefore, there are vested interests, moral or material, to be maintained, history is, of all the sciences or arts, that one most likely to suffer at the hands of those connected with such interests. Even where the truth will be of advantage to those interests, they are afraid of it, because the thorough discussion of it will involve the presentation of views disadvantageous to privilege.

Where, as is much more commonly the case (for vested interests, moral or material, are unreasoning and selfish things), the truth would certainly offend them, they are the more determined to prevent its appearance.

But of all vested interests none deal with such assured incomes, none are so immune by influence and tradition as the Universities.

Now, if the rich man has no temptation by way of popular fame, and the poor man no opportunity for endowment, in any branch of letters, there remains but a third form of support, and that is the support of the buying public. And the public will not buy.

I will suppose the case of a popular novelist, who in a few months shall write, not an historical novel, but a piece of so-called history. He shall call it, for instance, "England's Heroes." Before you tell me his name, or what he has written, I can tell you here and now what he will write on any number of points. He will call Hastings Senlac. In the Battle of Hastings he will make out Harold to be the head of a highly patriotic nation called the "Anglo-Saxons"; they shall be desperately defending themselves against certain French-speaking Scandinavians called Normans. He will deplore the defeat, but will say it was all for the best. Magna Charta he will have signed at Runnymede--probably he will have it drawn up there as well. He will translate the most famous clause by the modern words

"Judgment of his peers" and "law of the land." He will represent the Barons as having behind them the voice of the whole nation--and so forth. When he comes to Crécy he will make Edward III speak English. When he comes to Agincourt he will leave his readers as ignorant as himself upon the boundaries, numbers and power of the Burgundian faction. In the Civil War Oliver Cromwell will be an honest and not very rich gentleman of the middle-classes. The Parliamentary force will be that of the mass of the people against a few gallant but wicked aristocrats who follow the perfidious Charles. He will make no mention of the pay of the Ironsides. James II will be driven out by a popular uprising, in which the great Churchill will play an honourable and chivalric part. The loss of the American Colonies will be deplored, and will be ascribed to the folly of attempting to tax men of "Anglo-Saxon" blood, unless you grant them representation. The Continental troops will be treated as the descendants of Englishmen! The guns at Saratoga will be Colonial guns; the incapacity of the Fleet will not be touched upon. Here again, as in the case of the Battle of Hastings, all will be for the best, and there will be a few touching words upon the passionate affection now felt for Great Britain by the inhabitants of the United States. The defensive genius of Wellington will be represented as that of a general particularly great in the offensive. Talavera will be a victory. The Spanish Auxiliaries in the Peninsula will be contemptible. No guns will be abandoned before Coruña, but what are left at Coruña will be mentioned and re-embarked. The character of Nelson will receive a curious sort of glutinous praise; Emma Hamilton, not Naples, will be the stain upon his name; the Battle of Trafalgar will prevent the invasion of England.

This is a lengthy but not unjust description of what this gentleman would write; it is rubbish from beginning to end. It would sell, because every word of it would foster in the reader the illusion that the community of which he is a member is invincible under all circumstances, that effort and self-denial and suffering are spared him alone out of all mankind, and that a little pleasurable excitement, preferably that to be obtained from his favourite game, is the chief factor in military success.

I have omitted Alfred. Alfred in such a book will be the "teller of truth"--but he will not go to Mass.

Given that the name is sufficiently well known, there is hardly any limit to the sale of a book modelled upon these lines. Contrast with its fate the fate of a book, written no matter how powerfully, that should insist upon truths, no matter how valuable to the English people at the present moment. These truths need by no means be unpleasant, though at the present moment an unpleasant

71

truth is undoubtedly more valuable than a pleasant one. They could make as much or more for the glory of the country; they could be at any rate of infinitely greater service, but they would not be received, simply because they would compel close attention and brain-work in the reader as well as in the writer of them. An established groove would have to be abandoned; to use a strong metaphor, the reader would have to get out of bed, and that is what the modern reader will not do. Tell him that the men who fought on either side at Hastings' plain cared nothing for national but everything for feudal allegiance; that lex terrae means the local custom of ordeal and not the "law of the land"; tell him that judicium parium means the right of a noble to be judged by nobles, and has nothing to do with the jury system; tell him that Magna Charta was certainly drawn up before the meeting at Runnymede; that not until the Lancastrians did English kings speak English; that Oliver Cromwell owed his position to the enormous wealth of the Williamses, of whom had he not been a cadet, he would never have been known; tell him that the whole force of the Parliament resided in the squires and that the Civil Wars turned England into an oligarchy; tell him the exact truth about the infamy of Churchill; tell him what proportion of Englishmen during the American War were taxed without being represented; tell him what proportion of Washington's troops were of English blood; tell him any one illuminating and true thing about the history of his country, and the novelty will so offend him that a direct insult would have pleased him better.

What is true of history is true of nearly all the rest, and the upshot of the whole matter is that there is not, either in private patronage or in popular demand, a chance for history in modern England.

You can have excellent literature in journalism, and it will be widely read. I would say more--I would say that the better literature a newspaper admits, the more widely will that paper be read, or at any rate the greater will its influence be on modern Englishmen. But when it comes to the kneaded and wrought matter of the true Book, neither the public nor the centres of learning will have any of it, and the last medium which might make it possible, patronage, has equally disappeared, because the modern patron does not work in the daylight in the full view of the nation and with its full approbation, and he is no longer a public man (though he is richer than ever he was before). His patronage, therefore, though it is still considerable, is expended in satisfying his private demand. Private architects build him doubtful castles, private collectors get him manuscripts and jewels, but Letters, which are a public thing, he can no longer command.

It might be asked, by way of conclusion, whether there is any remedy for this state of things. There is none. Its prime cause resides in a certain attitude of the national mind, and this kind of broadly held philosophy is not changed save by slow preaching or external shock. As long as modern England remains what we know it, and follows the lines of change which we see it following, the Book will necessarily decline more and more, and we must make up our minds to it.

Of other evil tendencies of our time, one can say of some that they are obviously mending, of others that such and such an applicable remedy would mend them. Our public architecture is certainly getting better; so is our painting. Our gross and increasing contempt of self-government (to take quite another sphere) is curable by one or two simple reforms in procedure, registration, the expenses of election, and voting at the polls, which would restore the House of Commons to life, and give it power to express English will. But a regard for, a cultivation of, above all a sinking of wealth upon, English Letters is past praying for. We must wait until the tide changes; we can do nothing, and the waiting will be long.

José Maria de Heredia

The French have a phrase "la beauté du verbe" by which they would express a something in the sound and in the arrangement of words which supplements whatever mere thought those words were intended to express. It is evident that no definition of this beauty can be given, but it is also evident that without it letters would not exist. How it arises we cannot explain, yet the process is familiar to us in everything we do when we are attempting to fulfil an impulse towards whatever is good. An integration not of many small things but of an infinite series of infinitely small things build up the perfect gesture, the perfect line, the perfect intonation, and the perfect phrase. So indeed are all things significant built up: every tone of the voice, every arrangement of landscape or of notes in music which awake us and reveal the things beyond. But when one says that this is especially true of perfect expression one means that sometimes, rarely, the integration achieves a steadfast and sufficient formula. The mind is satisfied rather than replete. It asks no more; and if it desires to enjoy further the pleasure such completion has given it, it does not attempt to prolong or to develop the pleasure under which it has leapt; it is content to wait a while and to return, knowing well that it has here a treasure laid up for ever.

All this may be expressed in two words: the Classical Spirit. That is Classic of which it is true that the enjoyment is sufficient when it is terminated and that in the enjoyment of it an entity is revealed.

When men propose to bequeath to their fellows work of so supreme a kind it is to be noticed that they choose by instinct a certain material.

It has been said that the material in which he works affects the achievement of the artist: it is truer to say that it helps him. A man designing a sculpture in marble knows very well what he is about to do. A man attempting the exact and restrained rendering of tragedy upon the stage does not choose the stage as one among many methods, he is drawn to it: he needs it; the audience, the light, the evening, the very slope of the boards, all minister to his efforts. And so a man determined to produce the greatest things in verse takes up by nature exact and thoughtful words and finds that their rhythm, their combination, and their sound turn under his hand to something greater than he himself at first intended; he becomes a creator, and his name is linked with the name of a masterpiece. The material in which he has worked is hard; the price he has paid is an exceeding effect; the reward he has earned is permanence.

José de Heredia was an artist of this kind. The mass of the verse he produced, or rather published, was small. It might have been very large. It is not (as a foolish modern affectation will sometimes pretend) necessary to the endurance or even the excellence of work that it should be the product of exceptional moments; nor is it even true (as the wise Ancients believed) that great length of time must always mature it. But the small volume of Heredia's legacy to European letters does argue this at least in the poet, that he passionately loved perfection and that, finding himself able to achieve it (for perfection can be achieved) but now and then, he chose only to be remembered by the contentment which, now and then, his own genius had given him.

He worked upon verse as men work upon the harder metals; all that he did was chiselled very finely, then sawn to an exact configuration and at last inlaid, for when he published his completed volume it is true to say that every piece fitted in with the sound of one before and of one after. He was careful in the heroic degree.

His blood and descent are worthy of notice. He was a Spaniard, inheriting from the first Conquerors of the New World, nor was it remarkable to those who have received a proper enthusiasm for the classical spirit that the energy and even the violence natural to such a lineage should express themselves in the coldest and the most exalted form when, for the second time, a member of the family attempted verse. It is in the essence of that spirit that it alone can dare to be disciplined. It never doubts the motive power that will impel it; it is afraid, if anything, of an excess of power, and consciously imposes upon itself the limits which give it form.

Heredia in his person expressed the activity which impelled him, for he was strong, brown, erect, a rapid walker, and a man whose voice was perpetually modulated in resonant and powerful tones. In his last years during his administration of the Library at the Arsenal this vitality of his took on an aspect of good nature very charming and very fruitful. His organization of the place was thorough, his knowledge of the readers intimate. He refused the manuscripts of none, he advised, laughed, and consoled. His criticism was sure. Several, notably Marcel Prevost, were launched by his authority. The same deep security of literary judgment which had permitted him to chastise and to perfect his impeccable sonnets into their final form permitted him also to hold up before his eyes, grasp, and judge the work of every other man.

His frailty, as must always be the frailty of such men, was fastidiousness. The same sensitive consciousness which is said to

75

have all but lost us the Aeneid, and which certainly all but lost us the Apologia, dominated his otherwise vigorous soul. It is more than forty years since his first verse, written just upon achieving his majority, appeared in the old Revue de Paris and in the Revue des Deux Mondes. It was not till 1893 that he collected in one volume the scattered sonnets of his youth and middle age: the collection won him somewhat tardily his chair in the Academy. There is irony in the reminiscence that the man he defeated in that election was Zola.

All the great men who saluted his advent are dead. Théophile Gautier, who first established his fame; Hugo, who addressed to him, perhaps, that vigorous appeal in which strict labour is deified, and the medal and the marble bust are shown to outlive the greatest glories, are sometimes quoted as the last among the great French writers.

The immediate future will show that the stream of French excellence in this department, as in any other of human activity, is full, deep, and steady. The work of Heredia will help to prove it. He was a Spaniard, and a Colonial Spaniard. No other nation, perhaps, except the modern French, so inherit the romantic appetite of the later Roman Empire as to be able to mould and absorb every exterior element of excellence. It is remarkable that at the same moment Paris contemplated the funeral of the Italian de Brazza and the death of the Cuban Heredia. It is probable that those of us who are still young will live to see either name at the head of a new tradition. Heredia proved it possible not so much to imitate as to recapture the secure tradition of an older time. Perhaps the truest generalization that can be made with regard to the French people is to say that they especially in Western Europe (whose quality it is ever to transform itself but never to die) discover new springs of vitality after every period of defeat and aridity which they are compelled to cross. Heredia will prove in the near future a capital example of this power. He will increase silently in reputation until we, in old age, shall be surprised to find our sons and grandsons taking him for granted and speaking of him as one speaks of the Majores, of the permanent lights of poetry.

Normandy and the Normans

There is no understanding a country unless one gets to know the nature of its sub-units. In some way not easy to comprehend, impossible to define, and yet very manifest, each of the great national organisms of which Christendom is built up is itself a body of many regions whose differences and interaction endow it with a corporate life. No one could understand the past of England who did not grasp the local genius of the counties--Lancashire, cut off eastward by the Pennines, southward by the belt of marsh, with no natural entry save by the gate of Stockport; Sussex, which was and is a bishopric and a kingdom; Kent, Devon, the East Anglian meres. No one could (or does) understand modern England who does not see its sub-units to have become by now the great industrial towns, or who fails to seize the spirit of each group of such towns--with London lying isolated in the south, a negative to the rest.

France is built of such sub-units: it is the peculiarity of French development that these are not small territories mainly of an average extent with government answerable in a long day's ride to one centre, such as most English counties are; nor city States such as form the piles upon which the structure of Italy has been raised; nor kingdoms such as coalesced to reform the Spanish people; but provinces, differing greatly in area, from little plains enclosed, like the Rousillon, to great stretches of landscape succeeding landscape like the Bourbonnais or the Périgord.

The real continuity with an immemorial past which inspires all Gallic things is discoverable in this arrangement of Gaul. At the first glance one might imagine a French province to be a chance growth of the feudal ties and of the Middle Ages. A further effort of scholarship will prove it essentially Roman. An intimate acquaintance with its customs and with the site of its strongholds, coupled with a comparison of the most recent and most fruitful hypotheses of historians, will convince you that it is earlier than the Roman conquest; it is tribal, or the home of a group of cognate tribes, and its roots are lost in prehistory. So it is with Normandy.

This vast territory--larger (I think) than all North England from the Humber to Cheviot and from Chester to the Solway--has never formed a nation. It is typical of the national idea in France that Normandy should have "held" of the political centre of the country, probably since the first Gallic confederations were formed, certainly since the organization of the Empire. It is equally typical of the local life of a French province that, thus dependent, Normandy should have strictly preserved its manner and its spirit, and should have readily made war upon the Crown and resisted, as it still resists and will perhaps for ever, the centralizing forces of the national temper.

If you will travel day after day, and afoot, westward across the length of Normandy, you will have, if you are a good walker, a fortnight's task ahead of you; even if you are walking for a wager, a week's. It is the best way in which to possess a knowledge of that great land, and my advice would be to come in from the Picards over the bridge of Aumale across the little River Bresle (which is the boundary of Normandy to the east), and to go out by way of Pontorson, there crossing into Brittany over the little River Couesnon, which is the boundary of Normandy upon the west and beyond which lie the Bretons. In this way will you be best acquainted with the sharp differentiation of the French provinces passing into Normandy from Picardy, brick-built, horse-breeding, and slow, passing out of Normandy into the desolation and dreams of Brittany, and having known between the one and the other the chalk streams, the day-long beechen forests, the valley pastures, and the flamboyant churches of the Normans. You will do well to go by Neufchâtel, where the cheese is made, and by Rouen, then by Lisieux to Falaise, where the Conqueror was born, and thence by Vive to Avranches and so to the Breton border, taking care to choose the forests between one town and another for your road, since these many and deep woods--much wider than any we know in England-- are in great part the soul of the country.

By this itinerary you will not have taken all you should into view; you will not have touched the coast nor seen how Normandy is based upon the sea, and you will not have known the Cotentin, which is a little State of its own and is the quadrilateral which Normandy thrusts forth into the Channel. If you have the leisure, therefore, return by the north. Pass through Coutances and Valognes to Cherbourg, thence through Caen and Bayeux to the crossing of Seine at Honfleur, and then on by the chalk uplands and edges of the cliffs till you reach Eu upon the Bresle again. In such a double journey the character of the whole will be revealed, and if you have studied the past of the place before starting you will find your journey full. Avranches, Coutances, Lisieux, Bayeux, Rouen are not chance sites. Their great churches mark the bishoprics; the bishoprics in turn were the administrative centres of Rome, and Rome chose them because they were the strongholds or the sacred cities each of a Gallic tribe. The wealth of the valleys permitted everywhere that astonishing richness of detail which marks the stonework in village after village; the connexion with England, especially the last connexion under Henry V, explains the innumerable churches, splendid even in hamlets as are our own. The Bresle and the Couesnon, those little streams, are boundaries not of these last few centuries, but of a time beyond view; the Romans found them so. Diocletian made them the limits of the "Second Lyonesse," "Lugdunensis Secunda," which was the last Roman name of the province.

Here and there, near the west especially, you will discover names which recall the chief adventure of Normandy, the accident which baptized it with its Christian name, the landing of the Scandinavian pirates, the thousandth anniversary of which is now being celebrated. They came--we cannot tell in what numbers, some thousands--and harried the land. The old policy of the Empire, the policy already seven hundred years old, was had recourse to; the barbarians were granted settlement, inheritance, marriage, and partnership with the Lords of the Villae; their chief was permitted to hold local government, to tax and to levy men as the administrator of the whole province; but there followed something which wherever else the experiment had been tried had not followed: something of a new race arose. In Burgundy, in the northeast, in Visigothic Aquitaine the slight admixture of foreign blood had not changed the people, it was absorbed; the slight admixture of Scandinavian blood, coming so much later, in a time so degraded in government and therefore so open to natural influence, did change the Gallo-Romans of the Second Lyonesse. Few as the newcomers may have been in number, the new element transformed the mass, and when a century had permitted the union to work and settle, the great soldiers who founded us appeared. The Norman lords ordered, surveyed, codified, and ruled. They let Europe into England, they organized Sicily, they confirmed the New Papacy, they were the framework of the Crusades.

The phenomenon was brief. It lasted little more than a hundred years, but it transformed Europe and launched the Middle Ages. When it had passed, Normandy stood confirmed for centuries (and is still confirmed) in a character of its own. No longer adventurous but mercantile, apt, of a resisting courage, sober in thought, leaning upon tradition, not imperially but domestically strong: the country of Corneille and of Malesherbes, a reflection of that spirit in letters; the conservative body of to-day--for in our generation that is the mark of Normandy--and, in arms, the recruitment to which Napoleon addressed his short and famous order that "the Normans that day should do their duty."

The Old Things

Those who travel about England for their pleasure, or, for that matter, about any part of Western Europe, rightly associate with such travel the pleasure of history; for history adds to a man, giving him, as it were, a great memory of things--like a human memory, but stretched over a far longer space than that of one human life. It makes him, I do not say wise and great, but certainly in communion with wisdom and greatness.

It adds also to the soil he treads, for to this it adds meaning. How good it is when you come out of Tewkesbury by the Cheltenham road to look upon those fields to the left and know that they are not only pleasant meadows, but also the place in which a great battle of the mediaeval monarchy was decided, or as you stand by that ferry, which is not known enough to Englishmen (for it is one of the most beautiful things in England), and look back and see Tewkesbury tower, framed between tall trees over the level of the Severn, to see also the Abbey buildings in your eye of the mind--a great mass of similar stone with solid Norman walls, stretching on hugely to the right of the Minster.

All this historical sense and the desire to marry History with Travel is very fruitful and nourishing, but there is another interest, allied to it, which is very nearly neglected, and which is yet in a way more fascinating and more full of meaning. This interest is the interest in such things as lie behind recorded history, and have survived into our own times. For underneath the general life of Europe, with its splendid epic of great Rome turned Christian, crusading, discovering, furnishing the springs of the Renaissance, and flowering at last materially into this stupendous knowledge of today, the knowledge of all the Arts, the power to construct and to do--underneath all that is the foundation on which Europe is built, the stem from which Europe springs; and that stem is far, far older than any recorded history, and far, far more vital than any of the phenomena which recorded history presents.

Recorded history for this island and for Northern France and for the Rhine Valley is a matter of two thousand years; for the Western Mediterranean of three; but the things of which I speak are to be reckoned in tens of thousands of years. Their interest does not lie only nor even chiefly in things that have disappeared. It is indeed a great pleasure to rummage in the earth and find polished stones wrought by men who came so many centuries before us, and of whose blood we certainly are; and it is a great pleasure to find, or to guess that we find, under Canterbury the piles of a lake or marsh dwelling, proving that Canterbury has been there from all time; and that the apparently defenceless Valley City was once chosen as an impregnable site, when the water-meadows of the Stour were impassable as marsh, or with difficulty passable as a shallow lagoon. And it is delightful to stand on the earthwork a few miles west and to say to oneself (as one can say with a fair certitude), "Here was the British camp defending the south-east; here the tenth legion charged." All these are pleasant, but more pleasant, I think, to follow the thing where it actually survives.

Consider the track-ways, for instance. How rich is England in these! No other part of Europe will afford the traveller so permanent and so fascinating a problem. Elsewhere Rome hardened and straightened every barbaric trail until the original line and level disappeared; but in this distant province of Britain she could only afford just so much energy as made them a foothold for her soldiery; and all over England you can go, if you choose, foot by foot, along the ancient roads that were made by the men of your blood before they had heard of brick or of stone or of iron or of written laws.

I wonder that more men do not set out to follow, let us say, the Fosse-Way. There it runs right across Western England from the south-west to the north-east in a line direct yet sinuous, characters which are the very essence of a savage trail. It is a modern road for many miles, and you are tramping, let us say, along the Cotswold on a hard metalled modern English highway, with milestones and notices from the County Council telling you that the culverts will not bear a steam-engine, if so be you were to travel on one. Then suddenly this road comes up against a cross-road and apparently ceases, making what map draughtsmen call a "T"; but right in the same line you see a gate, and beyond it a farm lane, and so you follow. You come to a spinney where a ride has been cut through by the woodreeve, and it is all in the same line. The Fosse-Way turns into a little path, but you are still on it; it curves over a marshy brook-valley, picking out the firm land, and as you go you see old stones put there heaven knows how many (or how few) generations ago--or perhaps yesterday, for the tradition remains, and the country-folk strengthen their wet lands as they have strengthened them all these thousands of years; you climb up out of that depression, you get you over a stile, and there you are again upon a lane. You follow that lane, and once more it stops dead. This time there is a field before you. No right of way, no trace of a path, nothing but grass rounded into those parallel ridges which mark the modern decay of the corn lands and pasture--alas!--taking the place of ploughing. Now your pleasure comes in casting about for the trail; you look back along the line of the Way; you look forward in the same line till you find some indication, a boundary between two parishes, perhaps upon your map, or two or three quarries set together, or some other sign, and very soon you have picked up the line again.

So you go on mile after mile, and as you tread that line you have in the horizons that you see, in the very nature and feel of the soil beneath your feet, in the skies of England above you, the ancient purpose and soul of this Kingdom. Up this same line went the Clans marching when they were called Northward to the host; and up this went slow, creaking wagons with the lead of the Mendips or the tin of Cornwall or the gold of Wales.

And it is still there; it is still used from place to place as a high road, it still lives in modern England. There are some of its peers, as for instance the Ermine Street, far more continuous, and affording problems more rarely; others like the ridgeway of the Berkshire Downs, which Rome hardly touched, and of which the last two thousand years has, therefore, made hardly anything; you may spend a delightful day piecing out exactly where it crossed the Thames, making your guess at it, and wondering as you sit there by Streatley Vicarage whether those islands did not form a natural weir below which lay the ford.

The roads are the most obvious things. There are many more; for instance, thatch. The same laying of the straw in the same manner, with the same art, has continued, we may be certain, from a time long before the beginning of history. See how in the Fen Land they thatch with reeds, and how upon the Chalk Downs with straw from the Lowlands. I remember once being told of a record in a manor, which held of the Church and which lay upon the southern slope of the Downs, that so much was entered for "straw from the Lowlands": then, years afterwards, when I had to thatch a Bethlehem in an orchard underneath tall elms--a pleasant place to write in, with the noise of bees in the air--the man who came to thatch said to me: "We must have straw from the Lowlands; this upland straw is no good for thatching." Immediately when I heard him say this there was added to me ten thousand years. And I know another place in England, far distant from this, where a man said to me that if I wished to cross in a winter mist, as I had determined to do, Cross-Fell, that great summit of the Pennines, I must watch the drift of the snow, for there was no other guide to one's direction in such weather. And I remember another man in a little boat in the North Sea, as we came towards the Foreland, talking to me of the two tides, and telling me how if one caught the tide all the way up to

Long Nose and then went round it on the end of the flood, one caught a new tide up London river, and so made two tides in one day. He spoke with the same pleasure that silly men show when they talk about an accumulation of money. He felt wealthy and proud from the knowledge, for by this knowledge he had two tides in one day. Now knowledge of this sort is older than ten thousand years; and so is the knowledge of how birds fly, and of how they call, and of how the weather changes with the moon.

Very many things a man might add to the list that I am making. Dew-pans are older than the language or the religion; and the finding of water with a stick; and the catching of that smooth animal, the mole; and the building of flints into mortar, which if one does it in the old way (as you may see at Pevensey) the work lasts for ever, but if you do it in any new way it does not last ten years; then there is the knowledge of planting during the crescent part of the month, but not before the new moon shows; and there is the influence of the moon on cider, and to a less extent upon the brewing of ale; and talking of ale, the knowledge of how ale should be drawn from the brewing just when a man can see his face without mist upon the surface of the hot brew. And there is the knowledge of how to bank rivers, which is called "throwing the rives" in the South, but in the Fen Land by some other name; and how to bank them so that they do not silt, but scour themselves. There are these things and a thousand others. All are immemorial.

The Battle of Hastings

Related in the Manner of Oxford and Dedicated to that University

So careless were the French commanders (or more properly the French commander, for the rest were cowed by the bullying swagger of William) that the night, which should have been devoted to some sort of reconnaissance, if not of a preparation of the ground, was devoted to nothing more practical than the religious exercises peculiar to foreigners.

Their army, as we have seen, was not drawn from any one land, but it was in the majority composed of Normans and Bretons; we can therefore understand the extravagant superstition which must bear the blame for what followed.

Meanwhile, upon the heights above, the English host calmly prepared for battle. Fires were lit each in its appointed place, and at these meat was cooked under the stern but kindly eyes of the sergeant-majors. These also distributed at an appointed price liquor, of which the British soldier is never willing to be deprived, and as the hours advanced towards morning, the songs in which our adventurous race has ever delighted rose from the heights above the Brede.

The morning was misty, as is often the case over damp and marshy lands in the month of October, but the inclemency of the weather, or, to speak more accurately, the superfluous moisture precipitated from an already saturated atmosphere, was of no effect upon those silent and tenacious troops of Harold. It was far other with the so-called "Norman" host, who were full of forebodings-- only too amply to be justified--of the fate that lay before them upon the morrow.

It is curious to contrast the quiet skill and sagacity which marked the disposition of Harold with the almost childish simplicity of William's plan--if plan it may be called.

The Saxon hosts were drawn along the ridge in a position chosen with masterly skill. It afforded (as may still be seen) no dead ground for an attacking force and little cover. [1] Their left was arranged en potence, their right was drawn up in echelon. The centre followed the plan usual at that time, reposing upon the wings to its right and left and extended. The reserves were, of course, posted behind. Cavalry, as at Omdurman, played but a slight role in this typically national action and such mounted troops as were present seem to have been intermixed with the line in the fashion later known, in the jargon of the service, as "The Beggar's Quadrille." The Brigade of Guards is not mentioned in any record that I can discover, but was probably set by reversed companies in a square perpendicular to the main ravine and a little in front of the salient angle which appears upon the map at the point marked A.

The terrain can be clearly determined at the present day in spite of the changes that have taken place in the intervening years. It is a fairly steep slope of hemispherical contour interspersed with low bushes; the summit (upon which now stands our lovely English village of Battle and the residence of one of those cultured and leisured men who form the framework of our commonwealth) was then but a wild heath.

Harold himself could be distinguished in the centre of the line by his handsome features, restrained deportment, and unfailing gentlemanly good sense as he spoke to staff officer, orderly, and even groom with indefatigable skill.

In spite of the determination observable from a great distance upon the faces of the tall Saxon line, William with characteristic lack of balance opened the action by ordering a charge uphill with cavalry alone; it was a piece of tactics absurdly incongruous and one even he would never have attempted had he understood the foe that was before him, or the fate to which that foe had doomed him.

The lesson dealt him was as immediate as it was severe. The foreigners were thrust headlong down the hill, and a private letter tells us how the Men of Kent in particular buffeted the Normans about "as though they were boys." But even in the heat of this initial success Harold had the self-command to order the retirement upon the main position: and with troops such as his the order was equivalent to its execution.

This rude blow would have sufficed for any commander less vain than William, but he seems to have lost all judgment in a fit of personal vanity and to have ordered a second charge which could not but prove as futile as the first, delivered as it was up a perfect glacis strengthened by epaulements, reverses and countersunk galvon work and one whose natural strength was heightened by the stockade which the indomitable energy of Harold's troops had perfected in the early hours of the morning. Many of the stakes in this, the reader may note with pardonable pride, were of English oak--sharpened at the tip.

William's plan (if plan it may be called) was, as we have seen, necessarily futile and was foredoomed to failure. But Harold had no intention to let the action bear no more fruit than a tactical victory upon this particular field. The brain that had designed the exact

85

synchrony of Stamford Bridge and the famous march southward from the Humber was of that sort which is only found once in many centuries of the history of war and which is (it may be said without boasting) peculiar to this island.

Another general would have awaited the second charge with its useless butchery and still more useless contest for the barren name of victory. Not so Harold. Those commanding, cold grey eyes of his swept the line in a comprehensive glance, and though no written record of the detail remains, he must know little of the character of the man who does not understand that from Harold certainly proceeded the order for what followed.

The forces at the centre, which he commanded in person, deftly withdrew before the futile gallop of William's cavalry, leaving, with that coolness which has ever distinguished our troops, the laggards to their fate. At the same moment, and with marvellous precision, the left and right were withdrawn from the plateau rapidly and as by magic, and the old-fashioned tactics of mere impact (which William of Normandy seems seriously to have relied on!) were spent and wasted upon the now evacuated summit of the hill.

What followed is famous in history.

The cohesion of the Saxon force and the exactitude and coolness with which its great operation was performed is of good augury for the future of our country. Though it was now thick night, by no set road and with no cumbersome machinery of train and rear-guard, the whole of the vast assembly masked itself behind the woodlands of the Weald.

The Norman horsemen, bewildered and fatigued, gazed on the many that had fallen in defence of the masking position and wondered whether such novel happenings were victory or no, but the army whose concentration upon the Thames it was William's whole object to prevent, was already miles northward, each unit proceeding by exactly co-ordinated routes towards London.

There is perhaps no more difficult task set before soldiers than the quiet execution of such a manoeuvre after the heat of a heavy action, and none have performed it more magnificently than the veteran troop of Harold.

When (luckily) all the orders had been finally distributed a great tragedy marred the completeness of the day.

Just before the execution of this masterpiece of strategy, and as the autumn sun was sinking, the inevitable price which war demands of all its darlings was paid.

Harold himself, the artist of the great victory, fell. But we have no reason to believe that his loss retarded the retrograding movement in any degree. Men who create as Harold created have not their creations spoilt by death.

The shameful history of the close of the campaign is familiar to every schoolboy, and the military historian must be pardoned if he deals with a purely civilian blunder in a few brief words.

Parliament interfered--as it always does--with what should have been a matter for soldiers alone. Intrigues, bribery, or worse (with which the military historian has no concern) ruined what had been, in the field, one of the principal achievements of the Saxon arms. And William, who could not count to hold his own against regular forces and who was astonished to find himself free to retreat precipitately on Dover, was still more astonished to find himself accepted a few weeks later after an aimless march to the west and north by the politicians--or worse--at Berkhampstead. He and England were equally astounded to find that a broken and defeated invader could actually be accepted by the intriguers at Westminster and crowned King of England as the price of a secret bargain.

Such was the fruit of as great and successful an effort as ever Saxon soldier made: the Battle of Senlac: for such--as I am now free to reveal--was the true name of the field of action.

The ineptitude or avarice of politicians had undone the work of soldiers, and it is no wonder that the last of Harold's veterans, who retired in disgust to impregnable fortresses in Ely, Arthur's Seat, and Pudsey, are recorded to have gnashed their teeth and shed tears of indignation at the dispatches from the metropolis. At Crécy they were to be avenged.

The Roman Roads in Picardy

If a man were asked where he would find upon the map the sharpest impress of Rome and of the memories of Rome, and where he would most easily discover in a few days on foot the foundations upon which our civilization still rests, he might, in proportion to his knowledge of history and of Europe, be puzzled to reply. He might say that a week along the wall from Tyne to Solway would be the answer; or a week in the great Roman cities of Provence with their triumphal arches and their vast arenas and their Roman stone cropping out everywhere: in old quays, in ruined bridges, in the very pavement of the streets they use to-day, and in the columns of their living churches.

Now I was surprised to find myself after many years of dabbling in such things, furnishing myself the answer in quite a different place. It was in Picardy during the late manoeuvres of the French Army that, in the intervals of watching those great buzzing flies, the aeroplanes, and in the intervals of long tramps after the regiments or of watching the massed guns, the necessity for perpetually consulting the map brought home to me for the first time this truth--that Picardy is the province--or to be more accurate, Picardy with its marches in the Île de France, the edge of Normandy and the edge of Flanders--which retains to-day the most vivid impress of Rome. For though the great buildings are lacking, and the Roman work, which must here have been mainly of brick, has crumbled, and though I can remember nothing upstanding and patently of the Empire between the gate of Rheims and the frontier of Artois, yet one feature--the Roman road--is here so evident, so multiple, and so enduring that it makes up for all the rest.

One discovers the old roads upon the map, one after the other, with a sort of surprise. The scheme develops before one as one looks, and always when one thinks one has completed the web another and yet another straight arrow of a line reveals itself across the page.

The map is a sort of palimpsest. A mass of fine modern roads, a whole red blur of lanes and local ways, the big, rare black lines of the railway--these are the recent writing, as it were; but underneath the whole, more and more apparent and in greater and greater numbers as one learns to discover them, are the strict, taut lines which Rome stretched over all those plains.

There is something most fascinating in noting them, and discovering them one after the other.

For they need discovering. No one of them is still in complete use. The greater part must be pieced together from lengths of lanes which turn into broad roads, and then suddenly sink again into footpaths, rights of way, or green forest rides.

Often, as with our rarer Roman roads in England, all trace of the thing disappears under the plough or in the soft crossings of the river valleys; one marks them by the straightness of their alignment, by the place names which lie upon them (the repeated name Estree, for instance, which is like the place name "street" upon the Roman roads of England); by the recovery of them after a gap; by the discoveries which local archaeology has made.

Different men have different pastimes, and I dare say that most of those who read this will wonder that such a search should be a pastime for any man, but I confess it is a pastime for me. To discover these things, to recreate them, to dig out on foot the base upon which two thousand years of history repose, is the most fascinating kind of travel.

And then, the number of them! You may take an oblong of country with Maubeuge at one corner, Pontoise at another, Yvetot and some frontier town such as Fumes for the other two corners, and in that stretch of country a hundred and fifty miles by perhaps two hundred, you can build up a scheme of Roman ways almost as complete as the scheme of the great roads to-day.

That one which most immediately strikes the eye is the great line which darts upon Rouen from Paris.

Twice broken at the crossing of the river valleys, and lost altogether in the last twelve miles before the capital of Normandy, it still stands on the modern map a great modern road with every aspect of purpose and of intention in its going.

From Amiens again they radiate out, these roads, some, like the way to Cambray, in use every mile; some, like the old marching road to the sea, to the Portus Itius, to Boulogne, a mere lane often wholly lost and never used as a great modern road. This was the way along which the French feudal cavalry trailed to the disaster of Crécy, and just beyond Crécy it goes and loses itself in that exasperating but fascinating manner which is the whole charm of Roman roads wherever the hunter finds them. You may lay a ruler along this old forgotten track, all the way past Domqueur, Novelle (which is called Novelle-en-Chaussée, that is Novelle on the paved road), on past Estrée (where from the height you overlook the battlefield of Crécy), and that ruler so lying on your map points right at Boulogne Harbour, thirty odd miles away--and in all those thirty odd remaining miles I could not find another yard of it. But what an interest! What a hobby to develop! There is nothing like it in all the kinds of hunting that have ever been invented for filling up the whole of the mind. True, you will get no sauce of danger, but, on the other hand, you will hunt for weeks and weeks, and you will come back year after year and go on with your hunting, and sometimes you actually find--which is more than can be said for hunting some animals in the Weald.

How was it lost, this great main road of Europe, this marching road of the legions, linking up Gaul and Britain, the way that Hadrian went, and the way down which the usurper Constantine III must have come during that short adventure of his which lends such a romance to the end of the Empire? One cannot conceive why it should have disappeared. It is a sunken way down the hillside across the light railway which serves Crécy, it gets vaguer and vaguer, for all the world like those ridges upon the chalk that mark the Roman roads in England, and then it is gone. It leaves you pointing, I say, at that distant harbour, thirty odd miles off, but over all those miles it has vanished. The ghost of the legends cannot march along it any more. In one place you find a few yards of it about three miles south and east of Montreuil. It may be that the little lane leading into Estrée shows where it crossed the valley of the Cauche, but it is all guesswork, and therefore very proper to the huntsman.

Then there is that unbroken line by which St. Martin came, I think, when he rode into Amiens, and at the gate of the town cut his cloak in two to cover the beggar. It drives across country for Roye and on to Noyon, the old centre of the Kings. It is a great modern road all the way, and it stretches before you mile after mile after mile, until suddenly, without explanation and for no reason, it ends sharply, like the life of a man. It ends on the slopes of the hill called Choisy, at the edge of the wood which is there. And seek as you will, you will never find it again.

From that road also, near Amiens, branches out another, whose object was St. Quentin, first as a great high road, lost in the valley of the Somme, a lesser road again, still in one strict alignment, it reaches on to within a mile of Vermand, and there it stops dead. I do not think that between Vermand and St. Quentin you will find it. Go out north-westward from Vermand and walk perhaps five miles, or seven: there is no trace of a road, only the rare country lanes winding in and out, and the open plough of the rolling land. But continue by your compass so and you will come (suddenly again and with no apparent reason for its abrupt origin) upon the dead straight line that ran from the capital of the Nervii, three days' march and more, and pointing all the time straight at Vermand.

And so it is throughout the province and its neighbourhood.

Here and there, as at Bavai, a great capital has decayed. Here and there (but more rarely), a town wholly new has sprung up since the Romans, but the plan of the country is the same as that which they laid down, and the roads as you discover them, mark it out and establish it. The armies that you see marching to-day in their manoeuvres follow for half a morning the line which was taken by the Legions.

The Reward of Letters

It has often been remarked that while all countries in the world possess some sort of literature, as Iceland her Sagas, England her daily papers, France her prose writers and dramatists, and even Prussia her railway guides, one nation and one alone, the Empire of Monomotopa, is utterly innocent of this embellishment or frill.

No traveller records the existence of any Monomotopan quill-driver; no modern visitor to that delightful island has come across a littérateur whether in the worse or in the best hotels; and such reading as the inhabitants enjoy is entirely confined to works imported by large steamers from the neighbouring Antarctic Continent.

The causes of this singular and happy state of affairs were unknown (since the common histories did not mention them) until the recent discovery by Mr. Paley, the chief authority upon Monomotopan hieratic script, of a very ancient inscription which clearly sets forth the whole business.

It seems that an Emperor of Monomotopa, whose date can be accurately fixed by internal evidence to lie after the universal deluge and before the building of the Pyramid of Cheops, was, upon his accession to the throne, particularly concerned with the just repartition of taxes among his beloved subjects.

It would seem (if we are to trust the inscription) that in a past still more remote the taxes were so light that even the richest men would meet them promptly and without complaining, but this was at a period when the enemies of Monomotopa were at once distant and actively engaged in quarrelling among themselves. With sickening treachery these distant rival nations had determined to produce wealth and to live in amity, so that it was incumbent upon the Monomotopans not only to build ships, but actually to provide an army, and at last (what broke the camel's back) to establish fortifications of a very useless but expensive sort upon a dozen points of their Imperial coast.

Under the increasing strain the old fiscal system broke down. The poor were clearly embarrassed, as might be seen in their emaciated visages and from the terrible condition of their boots. The rich had reached the point after which it was inconvenient to them to pay any more. The middle classes were spending the greater part of their time in devising methods by which the exorbitant and intempestive demands of the collectors could be either evaded or, more rarely, complied with. In a word, a new and juster system of taxation was an imperative need, and the Emperor, who had just ascended the throne at the age of eighteen, and whom a sort of greenness had preserved from the iniquities of this world, was determined to effect the great reform.

With the advice of his Ministers (all of whom had had considerable experience in the handling of money), the Emperor at last determined that each man and woman should pay to the State one-tenth and no more of the wealth which he or she produced; those who produced nothing it was but common justice and reason to exempt, and the effect of this tardy act of justice upon the very rich was observed in the sudden increase of the death-rate from all those diseases that are the peculiar product of luxury and evil living. Paupers also, the unemployed, cripples, imbeciles, deaf mutes, and the clergy escaped under this beneficent and equable statute, and we may sum up the whole policy by saying that never was a law acclaimed with so much happy bewilderment nor subject to less expressed criticism than this.

It was, moreover, easy to estimate in this new fashion the total revenue of the State, since its produce had been accurately set down by statisticians of the utmost eminence, and one of these diverse documents had been taken for the basis of the new fiscal regime.

In practice also the collection was easy. Overseers would attend the harvest with large carts, prong the tenth turnip, hoick up the tenth sheaf of wheat, bucket out the tenth gallon of ale, and so forth. In the markets every tenth animal was removed by Imperial officers, every tenth newspaper was impounded as it left the press, and every tenth drink about to be consumed in the hostelries of the Empire was, after a simulacrum of proffering it, suddenly removed by the waiter and poured into a receptacle, the keys of which were very jealously guarded.

It was the same with the liberal professions: of the fee received by a barrister in the Criminal Courts a tenth was regularly demanded at the door when the verdict had been given and the prisoner whom he had defended passed out to execution. The tenth knock-out in the prize ring received by the professional pugilist was followed by the immediate sequestration of his fee for that particular encounter, and the tenth aria vibrating from the lips of a prima donna was either compounded for at a certain rate or taken in kind by the official who attended at every performance of grand opera.

One form of wealth alone puzzled the beneficent monarch and his Napoleonic advisers, and this was the production (for it then existed) of literary matter.

At first this seemed as simple to tax as any one of the other

93

numerous activities upon which the Emperor's loyal and loving subjects were engaged. A brief examination of the customs of the trade, conducted by an army of officials who penetrated into the very dens and attics in which Letters are evolved, reported that the method of payment was by the measurement of a number of words.

"It is, your Majesty," wrote the permanent official of the department in his minute, "the practice of those who charitably employ this sort of person to pay them in classes by the thousand words; thus one man gets one sequin a thousand, another two byzants, a third as much as a ducat, while some who have singularly attracted the notice of the public can command ten, twenty, nay forty scutcheons, and in some very exceptional cases a thousand words command one of those beautiful pieces of stiff paper which your Majesty in his bountiful provision tenders to his dutiful subjects for acceptance as metal under diverse penalties. The just taxation of these fellows can therefore be easily achieved if your Majesty, in the exercise of his almost superhuman wisdom, will but add a schedule to the Finance Act in which there shall be set down fifteen or twenty classes of writers, with their price per thousand words, and a compulsory registration of each class, enforced by the rude hand of the police."

The Emperor of Monomotopa immediately nominated a Royal Commission (unpaid), among whose sons, nephews, and private friends the salaried posts connected with the work were distributed. This Commission reported by a majority of one ere two years had elapsed. The schedule was designed, and such littérateurs as had not in the interval fled the country were registered, while a further enactment strictly forbidding their employers to make payment upon any other system completed the scheme.

But, alas! so full of low cunning and dirty dodges is this kind of man (I mean what we call authors) that very soon after the promulgation of the new law a marked deterioration in the quality of Monomotopan letters was apparent upon every side!

The citizen opening his morning paper would be astonished to find the leading article consist of nothing more original than a portion of the sacred Scriptures. A novel bought to ease the tedium of a journey would consist of long catalogues for the most part, and when it came to descriptions of scenery would fall into the most minute and detailed category of every conceivable feature of the landscape. Some even took advantage of the new regulation so far as to repeat one single word an interminable number of times, while it was remarked with shame by the Ministers of Religion that the morals of their literary friends permitted them only to use words of one syllable, and those of the shortest kind. And this they said was the only true and original Monomotopan dialect.

Such was the public inconvenience that next year a sharper and much more drastic law was passed, by which it was laid down that every literary composition should make sense within the meaning of the Act, and should be original so far as the reading of the judge appointed for the trial of the case extended. But though after the first few executions this law was generally observed, the nasty fellows affected by it managed to evade it in spirit, for by the use of obscure terms, of words drawn from dead languages, and of bold metaphor transferred from one art to another, they would deliberately invite prosecution, and then in the witness-box make fools of those plain men, the judge and jury, by showing that this apparently meaningless claptrap could, with sufficient ingenuity, be made to yield some sort of sense, and during this period no art critic was put to death.

Driven to desperation, the Emperor changed the whole basis of the Remuneration of Literary Labour, and ordered that it should be by the length of the prose or poetry measured in inches.

This reform, however, did but add to the confusion, for while the men of the pen wrote their works entirely in short dialogue, asterisks, and blanks, the publishers, who were now thoroughly organized, printed the same in smaller and smaller type, in order to avoid the consequences of the law.

At this last piece of insolence the Emperor's mind was quickly decided. Arresting one night not only all those who had ever written, but all those who had even boasted of letters, or who were so much as suspected by their relatives of secretly indulging in them, he turned the whole two million into a large but enclosed area, and (desiring to kill two birds with one stone) offered the ensuing spectacle as an amusement to the more sober and respectable sections of the community.

It is well known that the profession of letters breeds in its followers an undying hatred of each against his fellows. The public were therefore entertained for a whole day with the pleasing sight of a violent but quite disordered battle, in which each of the wretched prisoners seemed animated by no desire but the destruction of as many as possible of his hated rivals, until at last every soul of these detestable creatures had left its puny body and the State was rid of all.

A law which carried to the universities the rule of the primary schools--to wit, that men should be taught to read but not to write-- completed the good work. And there was peace.

The Eye-Openers

Without any doubt whatsoever, the one characteristic of the towns is the lack of reality in the impressions of the many: now we live in towns: and posterity will be astounded at us! It isn't only that we get our impressions for the most part as imaginary pictures called up by printer's ink--that would be bad enough; but by some curious perversion of the modern mind, printer's ink ends by actually preventing one from seeing things that are there; and sometimes, when one says to another who has not travelled, "Travel!" one wonders whether, after all, if he does travel, he will see the things before his eyes? If he does, he will find a new world; and there is more to be discovered in this fashion to-day than ever there was.

I have sometimes wished that every Anglo-Saxon who from these shores has sailed and seen for the first time the other Anglo-Saxons in New York or Melbourne, would write in quite a short letter what he really felt. Ninety-nine times out of a hundred men only write what they have read before they started, just as Rousseau in an eighteenth-century village believed that every English yokel could vote and that his vote conveyed a high initiative, making and unmaking the policy of the State; or just as people, hearing that the birth-rate of France is low, travel in that country and say they can see no children--though they would hardly say it about Sussex or Cumberland where the birth-rate is lower still.

What travel does in the way of pleasure (the providing of new and fresh sensations, and the expansion of experience), that it ought to do in the way of knowledge. It ought to and it does, with the wise, provide a complete course of unlearning the wretched tags with which the sham culture of our great towns has filled us. For instance, of Barbary--the lions do not live in deserts; they live in woods. The peasants of Barbary are not Semitic in appearance or in character; Barbary is full to the eye, not of Arab and Oriental buildings--they are not striking--but of great Roman monuments: they are altogether the most important things in the place. Barbary is not hot, as a whole: most of Barbary is extremely cold between November and March. The inhabitants of Barbary do not like a wild life, they are extremely fond of what civilization can give them, such as crème de menthe, rifles, good waterworks, maps, and railways: only they would like to have these things without the bother of strict laws and of the police, and so forth. Travel in Barbary with seeing eyes and you find out all this new truth.

Now it took the French forty years and more before each of these plain facts (and I have only cited half a dozen out of as many hundred) got into their letters and their print: they have not yet got into the letters and the print of other nations. But an honest man travelling in Barbary on his own account would pick up every one of these truths in two or three days, except the one about the lions; to pick up that truth you must go to the very edge of the country, for the lion is a shy beast and withdraws from men.

The wise man who really wants to see things as they are and to understand them, does not say: "Here I am on the burning soil of Africa." He says: "Here I am stuck in a snowdrift and the train twelve hours late"--as it was (with me in it) near Sétif in January, 1905. He does not say as he looks on the peasant at his plough outside Batna: "Observe yon Semite!" He says: "That man's face is exactly like the face of a dark Sussex peasant, only a little leaner." He does not say: "See those wild sons of the desert! How they must hate the new artificial world around them!" Contrariwise, he says: "See those four Mohammedans playing cards with a French pack of cards and drinking liqueurs in the café! See, they have ordered more liqueurs!" He does not say: "How strange and terrible a thing the railway must be to them!" He says: "I wish I was rich enough to travel first, for the natives pouring in and out of this third-class carriage, jabbering like monkeys, and treading on my feet, disturb my tranquillity. Some hundreds must have got in and out during the last fifty miles!"

In other words, the wise man has permitted eye-openers to rain upon him their full, beneficent, and sacramental influence. And if a man in travelling will always maintain his mind ready for what he really sees and hears, he will become a whole nest of Columbuses discovering a perfectly interminable series of new worlds.

A man can only talk of what he himself knows. Let me give further examples. I had always heard until I visited the Pyrenees how French civilization (especially in the matter of roads, motors, and things like that) went up to the "Spanish" frontier and then stopped dead. It doesn't. The change is at the Aragonese frontier. On the Basque third of the frontier the people are just as active and fond of wealth, and of scraping of stone and of cleanliness, and of drawing straight lines, to the north as to the south of it. They are all one people, as industrious, as thrifty, and as prosperous as the Scots. So are the Catalans one people, and you get much the same sort of advantages and disadvantages (apart from the effect of government) with the Catalans to the north as with the Catalans to the south of the border.

So with religion. I had thought to find the Spanish churches crowded. I found just the contrary. It was the French churches that were crowded, not the Spanish; and the difference between the truth--what one really sees and hears--and the printed legend happens to be very subtly illustrated in this case of religion. The French have inherited (and are by this time used to, and have, perhaps grown fond of) a big religious debate. Those who side with the national religion and tradition emphasize their opinion in every possible way--so do their opponents. You pick up two newspapers from Toulouse, for instance, and it is quite on the cards that the leading article of each will be a disquisition upon the philosophy of religion, the one, the "Depêche" of Toulouse, militantly, and often solently atheist; the other as militantly Catholic.

You don't get that in Pamplona, and you don't get it in Saragossa. What you get there is a profound dislike of being interfered with, ancient and lazy customs, wealth retained by the chapters, the monasteries, and the colleges, and with all this a curious, all-pervading indifference.

One might end this little train of thought by considering a converse test of what the eye-opener is in travel; and that test is to talk to foreigners when they first come to England and see how they tend to discover in England what they have read of at home instead of what they really see. There have been very few fogs in London of late, but your foreigner nearly always finds London foggy. Kent does not show along its main railway line the evidence of agricultural depression: it is like a garden. Yet, in a very careful and thorough French book just published by a French traveller, his bird's-eye view of the country as he went through Kent just after landing would make you think the place a desert; he seems to have thought the hedges a sign of agricultural decay. The same foreigner will discover a plebeian character in the Commons and an aristocratic one in the House of Lords, though he shall have heard but four speeches in each, and though every one of the eight speeches shall have been delivered by members of one family group closely intermarried, wealthy, titled, and perhaps (who knows?) of some lineage as well.

The moral is that one should tell the truth to oneself, and look out for it outside one. It is quite as novel and as entertaining as the discovery of the North Pole--or, in case that has come off (as some believe), the discovery of the South Pole.

The Public

I notice a very curious thing in the actions particularly of business men to-day, and of other men also, which is the projection outward from their own inward minds of something which is called "The Public"--and which is not there.

I do not mean that a business man is wrong when he says that "the public will demand" such and such an article, and on producing the article finds it sells widely; he is obviously and demonstrably right in his use of the word "public" in such a connexion. Nor is a man wrong or subject to illusion when he says, "The public have taken to cinematograph shows," or "The public were greatly moved when the Hull fishermen were shot at by the Russian fleet in the North Sea." What I mean is "The Public" as an excuse or scapegoat; the Public as a menace; the Public as a butt. That Public simply does not exist.

For instance, the publisher will say, as though he were talking of some monster, "The Public will not buy Jinks's work. It is first-class work, so it is too good for the Public." He is quite right in his statement of fact. Of the very small proportion of our people who read only a fraction buy books, and of the fraction that buy books very few indeed buy Jinks's. Jinks has a very pleasant up-and-down style. He loves to use funny words dragged from the tomb, and he has delicate little emotions. Yet hardly anybody will buy him--so the publisher is quite right in one sense when he says, "The Public" won't buy Jinks. But where he is quite wrong and suffering from a gross illusion is in the motive and the manner of his saying it. He talks of "The Public" as something gravely to blame and yet irredeemably stupid. He talks of it as something quite external to himself, almost as something which he has never personally come across. He talks of it as though it were a Mammoth or an Eskimo. Now, if that publisher would wander for a moment into the world of realities he would perceive his illusion. Modern men do not like realities, and do not usually know the way to come in contact with them. I will tell the publisher how to do so in this case.

Let him consider what books he buys himself, what books his wife buys; what books his eldest son, his grandmother, his Aunt Jane, his old father, his butler (if he runs to one), his most intimate friend, and his curate buy. He will find that not one of these people buys Jinks. Most of them will talk Jinks, and if Jinks writes a play, however dull, they will probably go and see it once; but they draw the line at buying Jinks's books--and I don't blame them.

The moral is very simple. You yourselves are "The Public," and if you will watch your own habits you will find that the economic explanation of a hundred things becomes quite clear.

I have seen the same thing in the offices of a newspaper. Some simple truth of commanding interest to this country, involving no attack upon any rich man, and therefore not dangerous under our laws, comes up for printing. It is discussed in the editor's room. The editor says, "Yes, of course, we know it is true, and of course it is important, but the Public would not stand it."

I remember one newspaper office of my youth in which the Public was visualized as a long file of people streaming into a Wesleyan chapel, and another in which the Public was supposed to be made up without exception of retired officers and maiden ladies, every one of whom was a communicant of the English Established Church, every one of good birth, and yet every one devoid of culture.

Without the least doubt each of these absurd symbols haunted the brain of each of the editors in question. The editor of the first paper would print at wearisome length accounts of obscure Catholic clerical scandals on the Continent, and would sweat with alarm if his sub-editors had admitted a telegram concerning the trial of some fraudulent Protestant missionary or other in China.

Meanwhile his rather dull paper was being bought by you and me, and bank clerks and foreign tourists, and doctors, and publicans, and brokers, Catholics, Protestants, atheists, "peculiar people," and every kind of man for many reasons--because it had the best social statistics, because it had a very good dramatic critic, because they had got into the habit and couldn't stop, because it came nearest to hand on the bookstall. Of a hundred readers, ninety-nine skipped the clerical scandal and either chuckled over the fraudulent missionary or were bored by him and went on to the gambling news from the Stock Exchange. But the type for whom all that paper was produced, the menacing god or demon who was supposed to forbid publication of certain news in it, did not exist.

So it was with the second paper, but with this difference, that the editor was right about the social position of those who read his sheet, but quite wrong about the opinions and emotions of people in that social position.

It was all the more astonishing from the fact that the editor was born in that very class himself and perpetually mixed with it. No one perhaps read "The Stodge" (for under this device would I veil the true name of the organ) more carefully than those retired officers of either service who are to be found in what are called our "residential" towns. The editor was himself the son of a colonel of guns who had settled down in a Midland watering-place. He ought to have known that world, and he did know that world, but he kept his illusion of his Public quite apart from his experience of realities.

Your retired officer (to take his particular section of this particular paper's audience) is nearly always a man with a hobby, and usually a good scientific or literary hobby at that. He writes many of our best books demanding research. He takes an active part in public work which requires statistical study. He is always a travelled man, and nearly always a well-read man. The broadest and the most complete questioning and turning and returning of the most fundamental subjects--religion, foreign policy, and domestic economics--are quite familiar to him. But the editor was not selecting news for that real man; he was selecting news for an imaginary retired officer of inconceivable stupidity and ignorance, redeemed by a childlike simplicity. If a book came in, for instance, on biology, and there was a chance of having it reviewed by one of the first biologists of the day, he would say: "Oh, our Public won't stand evolution," and he would trot out his imaginary retired officer as though he were a mule.

Artists, by which I mean painters, and more especially art critics, sin in this respect. They say: "The public wants a picture to tell a story," and they say it with a sneer. Well, the public does want a picture to tell a story, because you and I want a picture to tell a story. Sorry. But so it is. The art critic himself wants it to tell a story, and so does the artist. Each would rather die than admit it, but if you set either walking, with no one to watch him, down a row of pictures you would see him looking at one picture after another with that expression of interest which only comes on a human face when it is following a human relation. A mere splash of colour would bore him; still more a mere medley of black and white. The story may have a very simple plot; it may be no more than an old woman sitting on a chair, or a landscape, but a picture, if a man can look at it all, tells a story right enough. It must interest men, and the less of a story it tells the less it will interest men. A good landscape tells so vivid a story that children (who are unspoilt) actually transfer themselves into such a landscape, walk about in it, and have adventures in it.

They make another complaint against the public, that it desires painting to be lifelike. Of course it does! The statement is accurate, but the complaint is based on an illusion. It is you and I and all the world that want painting to imitate its object. There is a wonderful picture in the Glasgow Art Gallery, painted by someone a long time ago, in which a man is represented in a steel cuirass with a fur tippet over it, and the whole point of that picture is that the fur looks like fur and the steel looks like steel. I never met a critic yet

101

who was so bold as to say that picture was a bad picture. It is one of the best pictures in the world; but its whole point is the liveliness of the steel and of the fur.

Finally, there is one proper test to prove that all this jargon about "The Public" is nonsense, which is that it is altogether modern. Who quarrelled with the Public in the old days when men lived a healthy corporate life, and painted, wrote, or sang for the applause of their fellows?

If you still suffer from the illusion after reading these magisterial lines of mine, why, there is a drastic way to cure yourself, which is to go for a soldier; take the shilling and live in a barracks for a year; then buy yourself out. You will never despise the public again. And perhaps a better way still is to go round the Horn before the mast. But take care that your friends shall send you enough money to Valparaiso for your return journey to be made in some comfort; I would not wish my worst enemy to go back the way he came.

On Entries

I am always planning in my mind new kinds of guide books. Or, rather, new features in guide books.

One such new feature which I am sure would be very useful would be an indication to the traveller of how he should approach a place.

I would first presuppose him quite free and able to come by rail or by water or by road or on foot across the fields, and then I would describe how the many places I have seen stand quite differently in the mind according to the way in which one approaches them.

The value of travel, to the eye at least, lies in its presentation of clear and permanent impressions, and these I think (though some would quarrel with me for saying it) are usually instantaneous. It is the first sharp vision of an unknown town, the first immediate vision of a range of hills, that remains for ever and is fruitful of joy within the mind, or, at least, that is one and perhaps the chief of the fruits of travel.

I remember once, for instance, waking from a dead sleep in a train (for I was very tired) and finding it to be evening. What woke me was the sudden stopping of the train. It was in Italy. A man in the carriage said to me that there was some sort of accident and that we should be waiting a while. The people got out and walked about by the side of the track. I also got out of the carriage and took the air, and when I so stepped out into the cool of that summer evening I was amazed at the loneliness and tragedy of the place.

There were no houses about me that I could see save one little place built for the railway men. There was no cultivation either.

Close before me began a sort of swamp with reeds which hardly moved to the air, and this gradually merged into a sheet of water above and beyond which were hills, barren and not very high, which took the last of the daylight, for they looked both southward and to the west. The more I watched the extraordinary and absolute scene the less I heard of the low voices about me, and indeed a sort of positive silence seemed to clothe the darkening landscape. It was full of something quite gone down, and one had the impression that it would never be disturbed.

As the light lessened, the hills darkened, the sky took on one broad and tender colour, the sheet of water gleamed quite white, and the reeds stood up like solid shadows against it. I wish I could express in words the impression of recollection and of savage

103

mourning which all that landscape imposed, but from that impression I was recalled and startled by the guard, who came along telling us that things were righted and that the train would start again; soon we were in our places and the rapid movement isolated for me the memory of a singularly vivid scene. I thought the place must have a name, and I asked a neighbour in the carriage what it was called; he told me it was called Lake Trasimene.

Now I do not say that this tragic site is to be visited thus. It was but an accident, though an accident for which I am most grateful to my fate. But what I have said here illustrates my meaning that the manner of one's approach to any place in travel makes all the difference.

Thus one may note how very different is Europe seen from the water than seen from any other opportunity for travel. So many of the great cathedrals were built to dominate men who should watch them from the wharves of the mediaeval towns, but I think it is almost a rule if you have leisure and can take your choice to choose this kind of entry to them. Amiens is quite a different thing seen from the river below it to the north and east from what it is seen by a gradual approach along the street of a modern town. The roofs climb up at it, and it stands enthroned. So Chartres seen from the little Eure; but the Eure is so small a river that he would be a bold man who would travel up it all this way. Nevertheless it is a good piece of travel, and anyone who will undertake it will see Louviers and will pass Anet, where the greatest work of the Renaissance once stood, and will go through lonely but rich pastures until at last he gets to Chartres by the right gate. Thence he will see something astonishing for so flat a region as the Beauce. The great church seems mountainous upon a mountain. Its apse completes the unclimbable steepness of the hill and its buttresses follow the lines of the fall of it. But if you do not come in by the river, at least come in by the Orleans road. I suppose that nine people out of ten, even to-day when the roads are in proper use again, come into Chartres by that northern railway entry, which is for all the world like coming into a great house by a big, neglected backyard.

Then if ever you have business that takes you to Bayonne, come in by river and from the sea, and how well you will understand the little town and its lovely northern Gothic!

Some of the great churches all the world knows must be seen from the water, and most of the world so sees them. Ely is one, Cologne is another, but how many people have looked right up at Durham as at a cliff from that gorge below, or how many have seen the height of Albi from the Tarn?

As for famous cities with their walls, there is no doubt that a man should approach them by the chief high road, which once linked them with their capital, or with their nearest port, or with Rome--and that although this kind of entry is nowadays often marred by ugly suburbs. You will get much your finest sight of Segovia as you come in by the road from the Guadarama and from Madrid. It is from that point that you were meant to see the town, and you will get much your best grip on Carcassonne, old Carcassonne, if you come in by the road from Toulouse at morning as you were meant to come, and so Coucy should be approached by that royal road from Soissons and from the south, while as for Laon (the most famous of the hill towns), come to it from the east, for it looks eastward, and its lords were Eastern lords.

Ranges of hills, I think, are never best first seen from railways. Indeed, I can remember no great sight of hills so seen, not even the Alps. A railway must of necessity follow the floor of the valley and tunnel and creep round the shoulders of the bulwarks. There is perhaps one exception to this rule, which is the sight of the Pyrenees from the train as one comes into Tarbes. It is a wise thing if you are visiting those hills to come into Tarbes by night and sleep there, and then next morning the train upon its way to Pau unfolds you all the wall of the mountains. But this is an accident. It is because the railway runs upon a sort of high platform that you see the mountains so. With all other hills that I remember it is best to have them burst suddenly upon you from the top of some pass lifted high above the level and coming, let us say, to a height half their own. Certainly the Bernese Oberland is more wonderful caught in one moment from the Jura than introduced in any other way, and the snows on Atlas over the desert seem like part of the sky when they come upon one after climbing the red rocks of the high plateaux and you see them shining over the salt marshes. The Vosges you cannot thus see from a half-height; there is no platform, and that is perhaps why the Vosges have not impressed travellers as they should. But you can so watch the grand chain of old volcanoes which are the rampart of Auvergne. You can stand upon the high wooden ridge of Foreze and see them take the morning across the mists and the flat of the Limagne, where the Gauls fought Caesar. Further south from the high table of the Velay you can see the steep backward escarpment of the Cevennes, inky blue, desperately blue, blue like nothing else on earth except the mountains in those painters of North Italy, of the parts north and east of Venice, the name of whose school escapes me--or, rather, I never knew it.

Now, as for towns that live in a hollow, it is great fun to come upon them from above. They are not used to being thus taken at a disadvantage and they are both surprised and surprising. There are many towns in holes and trenches of Europe which you can thus play "peep-bo" with if you will come at them walking. By train they will mean nothing to you. You will probably come upon them out of a long, shrieking tunnel, and by the high road they mean little more, for the high road will follow the vale. But if you come upon them from over their guardian cliffs and scars you catch them unawares, and this is a good way of approaching them, for you master them, as it were, and spy them out before you enter in. You can act thus with Grenoble and with many a town on the Meuse, and particularly with Aubusson, which lies in the depths of so dreadful a trench that I could wonder how man ever dreamt of living and building there.

The most difficult of all places on which to advise, I think, would be the very great cities, the capitals. They seem to have to-day no noble entries and no proper approach. Perhaps we shall only deal with them justly when we can circle down to them through the air and see their vast activity splashed over the plain. Anyhow, there is no proper way of entering them now that I know of. Berlin is not worth entering at all. Rome (a man told me once) could be entered by some particular road over the Janiculum, I think--which also, if I remember right, was the way that Shelley came--but I despair of Paris, and certainly of London. I cannot even recall an entry for Brussels, though Brussels is a monumental city with great rewards for those who love the combination of building and hills.

Perhaps, after all, the happiest entries of all and the most easy are those of our many market towns, small and not swollen in Britain and in Northern Gaul and in the Netherlands and in the Valley of the Rhine. These hardly ever fail us, and we come upon them in our travels as they desire that we should come, and we know them properly as things should properly be known--that is, from the beginning.

Companions of Travel

I write of travelling companions in general, and not in particular, making of them a composite photograph, as it were, and finding what they have in common and what is their type; and in the first place I find them to be chance men. For there are some people who cannot travel without a set companion who goes with them from Charing Cross all over the world and back to Charing Cross again. And there is a pathos in this: as Balzac said of marriage, "What a commentary on human life, that human beings must associate to endure it." So it is with many who cannot endure to travel alone: and some will positively advertise for another to go with them.

In a glade of the Sierra Nevada, which, for awful and, as it were, permanent beauty seemed not to be of this world, I came upon a man slowly driving along the trail a ramshackle cart, in which were a few chairs and tables and bedding. He had a long grey beard and wild eyes; he was old, and very small like a gnome, but he had not the gnome's good-humour. I asked him where he was going, and I slowed down, so as to keep pace with his ridiculous horse. For some time he would not answer me, and then he said, "Out of this." He added, "I am tired of it." And when I asked him, "Of what?" his only answer was an old-fashioned oath. But from further complaints which he made I gathered that what he was tired of was clearing forests, digging ground, paying debts, and in general living upon this unhappy earth. He did not like me very much, and though I would willingly have learned more, he would tell me nothing further, so when we got to a place where there was a little stream I went on and left him.

I have never forgotten the sadness of this man. Where he was going, and what he expected to do, or what opportunities he had, I have never understood. Though some years after, in quite another place--namely, Steyning, in Sussex--I came upon just such another, whose quarrel was with the English climate, the rich and the poor, and the whole constitution of God's earth. These are the advantages of travel, that one meets so many men whom one would otherwise never meet, and that one feeds as it were upon the complexity of mankind.

Thus in a village called Encamps, in the depths of Andorra, where no man has ever killed another, I found a man with a blue face, who was a fossil, the kind of man you would never find in the swelling life of Western Europe. He was emancipated, he had studied in Perpignan, over and beyond the great hills. He could not see why he should pay taxes to support a priest. "The priests" he assured me, "say the most ridiculous things. They narrate the most impossible fables. They affirm what cannot possibly be true. All that they say is in opposition to science. If I am ill, can a priest cure me? No. Can a priest tell me how to build, or how to light my house? He is unable to do so. He is a useless and a lying mouth, why should I feed him?"

I questioned this man very closely, and discovered that in his view the world slowly changed from worse to better, and to accelerate this process enlightenment alone was needed. "But what do these brutes," he said, alluding to his fellow-countrymen, "know of enlightenment? They do not even make roads, because the priests forbid them."

I could write at length upon this man. He was not a Sceptic as you may imagine, nor had he adopted the Lucretian form of Epicureanism. Not a bit of it. He was a hearty Atheist, with Positivist leanings. I further found that he had married a woman older, wealthier, and if possible uglier than himself. She kept the inn, and was very kind to him. His life would have been quite happy had he not been tortured by the monstrous superstitions of others.

Then, again, in the town of Marseilles, only two years ago, I met a man who looked well fed, and had a stalwart, square French face, and whose politico-economic ideal, though it was not mine, greatly moved me. It was just past midnight, and I was throwing little stones into the old Greek harbour, the stench and the glory of which are nearly three thousand years old; I was to be off at dawn upon a tramp steamer, and I had so determined to pass the few hours of darkness.

I was throwing pebbles into the water, I say, and thinking about Ulysses, when this man came slouching up, with his hands in the pockets of his enormous corduroy trousers, and, looking at me with some contempt from above (for he was standing, I was sitting), he began to converse with me. We talked first of ships, then of heat and cold, and so on to wealth and poverty; and thus it was I came upon his views, which were that there should be a sort of break up, and houses ought to be burned, and things smashed, and people killed; and over and above this, it should be made plain that no one had a right to govern: not the people, because they were always being bamboozled; obviously not the rich; least of all, the politicians, to whom he justly applied the most derogatory epithets. He waved his arm out in the darkness at the Phoceans, at the half-million of Marseilles, and said, "All that should disappear." The constructive side of his politico-economic scheme was negative. He

108

was a practical man. None of your fine theories for him. One step at a time. Let there be a Chambardement--that is, a noisy collapse, and he would think about what to do afterwards.

His was not the narrow, deductive mind. He was objective and concrete. Believe me or not, he was paid an excellent wage by the municipality to prevent people like me, who sit up at night, from doing mischief in the harbour. When I had come to an end of his politico-economic scheme--the main lines of which were so clear and simple that a child could understand them--we fell to talking of the tides, and I told him that in my country the sea went up and down. He was no rustic, and would have no such commonplace truths. He was well acquainted with the Phenomenon of the Tides; it was due to the combined attraction of the sun and of the moon. But when I told him I knew places where the tides fell thirty or forty feet, we would have had a violent quarrel had I not prudently admitted that that was romantic exaggeration, and that five or six was the most that one ever saw it move. I avoided the quarrel, but the little incident broke up our friendship, and he shuffled away. He did not like having his leg pulled.

There are many others I remember. Those I have written about elsewhere I am ashamed to recall, as the man at Jedburgh, who first expounded to me how one knew all about the fate of the individual soul, and then objected to personal questions about his own; the German officer man at Aix-la-Chapelle, who had hair the colour of tow, and gave me minute details of the method by which England was to be destroyed; a man I met upon the Appian Way, who told the most abominable lies; and another man who met me outside Oxford station during the Vac. and offered to show me the sights of the town for a consideration, which he did, but I would not pay him because he was inaccurate, as I easily proved by a few searching questions upon the exact site of Bocardo (of which he had never heard), and the negative evidence against a Roman origin for the site of the city. Moreover, he said that Trinity was St. John's, which was rubbish.

Then there was another man who travelled with me from Birmingham, pressed certain tracts upon me, and wanted to charge me sixpence each at Paddington. But if I were to speak of even these few I should exceed.

On the Sources of Rivers

There are certain customs in man the permanence of which gives infinite pleasure. When the mood of the schools is against them these customs lie in wait beneath the floors of society, but they never die, and when a decay in pedantry or in despotism or in any other evil and inhuman influence permits them to reappear they reappear.

One of these customs is the religious attachment of man to isolated high places, peaks, and single striking hills. On these he must build shrines, and though he is a little furtive about it nowadays, yet the instinct is there, strong as ever. I have not often come to the top of a high hill with another man but I have seen him put a few stones together when he got there, or, if he had not the moral courage so to satisfy his soul, he would never fail on such an occasion to say something ritual and quasi-religious, even if it were only about the view; and another instinct of the same sort is the worship of the sources of rivers.

The Iconoclast and the people whose pride it is that their senses are dead will see in a river nothing more than so much moisture gathered in a narrow place and falling as the mystery of gravitation inclines it. Their mood is the mood of that gentleman who despaired and wrote:

> A cloud's a lot of vapour,
> The sky's a lot of air,
> And the sea's a lot of water
> That happens to be there.

You cannot get further down than that. When you have got as far down as that all is over. Luckily God still keeps his mysteries going for you, and you can't get rid, even in that mood, of the certitude that you yourself exist and that things outside of you are outside of you. But when you get into that modern mood you do lose the personality of everything else, and you forget the sanctity of river heads.

You have lost a great deal when you have forgotten that, and it behoves you to recover what you have lost as quickly as possible, which is to be done in this way: Visit the source of some famous stream and think about it. There was a Scotchman once who discovered the sources of the Nile, to the lasting advantage of mankind and the permanent glory of his native land. He thought the

110

source of the Nile looked rather like the sources of the Till or the Tweed or some such river of Thule. He has been ridiculed for saying this, but he was mystically very right. The source of the greatest of rivers, since it was sacred to him, reminded him of the sacred things of his home.

When I consider the sources of rivers which I have seen, there is not one, I think, which I do not remember to have had about it an influence of awe. Not only because one could in imaginings see the kingdoms of the cities which it was to visit and the way in which it would bind them all together in one province and one story, but also simply because it was an origin.

The sources of the Rhone are famous: the Rhone comes out of a glacier through a sort of ice cave, and if it were not for an enormous hotel quite four-square it would be as lonely a place as there is in Europe, and as remarkable a beginning for a great river as could anywhere be found. Nor, when you come to think of it, does any European river have such varied fortunes as the Rhone. It feeds such different religions and looks on such diverse landscapes. It makes Geneva and it makes Avignon; it changes in colour and in the nature of its going as it goes. It sees new products appearing continually on its journey until it comes to olives, and it flows past the beginning of human cities, when it reflects the huddle of old Arles.

The sources of the Garonne are well known. The Garonne rises by itself in a valley from which there is no issue, like the fabled valleys shut in by hills on every side. And if it were anything but the Garonne it would not be able to escape: it would lie imprisoned there for ever. Being the Garonne it tunnels a way for itself right under the High Pyrenees and comes out again on the French side. There are some that doubt this, but then there are people who would doubt anything.

The sources of the River Arun are not so famous as these two last, and it is a good thing, for they are to be found in one of the loneliest places within an hour of London that any man can imagine, and if you were put down there upon a windy day you would think yourself upon the moors. There is nothing whatsoever near you at the beginnings of the little sacred stream.

Thames had a source once which was very famous. The water came out plainly at a fountain under a bleak wood just west of the Fosse Way, under which it ran by a culvert, a culvert at least as old as the Romans. But when about a hundred years ago people began to improve the world in those parts, they put up a pumping station and they pumped Thames dry--since which time its gods have deserted the river.

The sources of the Ribble are in a lonely place up in a corner of the hills where everything has strange shapes and where the rocks make one think of trolls. The great frozen Whernside stands up above it, and Ingleborough Hill, which is like no other hill in England, but like the flat-topped Mesas which you have in America, or (as those who have visited it tell me) like the flat hills of South Africa; and a little way off on the other side is Pen-y-ghent, or words to that effect. The little River Ribble rises under such enormous guardianship. It rises quite clean and single in the shape of a little spring upon the hillside, and too few people know it. The other river that flows east while the Ribble flows west is the River Ayr. It rises in a curious way, for it imitates the Garonne, and finding itself blocked by limestone burrows underneath at a place called Malham Tarn, after which it has no more trouble.

The River Severn, the River Wye, and a third unimportant river, or at least important only for its beauty (and who would insist on that?) rise all close together on the skirts of Plinlimmon, and the smallest of them has the most wonderful rising, for it falls through the gorge of Llygnant, which looks like, and perhaps is, the deepest cleft in this island, or, at any rate, the most unexpected. And a fourth source on the mountain, a tarn below its summit, is the source of Rheidol, which has a short but adventurous life like Achilles.

There is one source in Europe that is properly dealt with, and where the religion due to the sources of rivers has free play, and this is the source of the Seine. It comes out upon the northern side of the hills which the French call the Hills of Gold, in a country of pasturage and forest, very high up above the world and thinly peopled. The River Seine appears there in a sort of miraculous manner, pouring out of a grotto, and over this grotto the Parisians have built a votive statue; and there is yet another of the hundred thousand things that nobody knows.

On Error

There is an elusive idea that has floated through the minds of most of us as we grew older and learnt more and more things. It is an idea extremely difficult to get into set terms. It is an idea very difficult to put so that we shall not seem nonsensical; and yet it is a very useful idea, and if it could be realized its realization would be of very practical value. It is the idea of a Dictionary of Ignorance and Error.

On the face of it a definition of the work is impossible. Strictly speaking it would be infinite, for human knowledge, however far extended, must always be infinitely small compared with all possible knowledge, just as any given finite space is infinitely small compared with all space.

But that is not the idea which we entertain when we consider this possible Dictionary of Ignorance and Error. What we really mean is a Dictionary of the sort of Ignorance and the sort of Error which we know ourselves to have been guilty of, which we have escaped by special experience or learning as time went on, and against which we would warn our fellows.

Flaubert, I think, first put it down in words, and said that such an encyclopaedia was very urgently needed.

It will never exist, but we all know that it ought to exist. Bits of it appear from time to time piecemeal and here and there, as for instance in the annotations which modern scholarship attaches to the great text, in the printed criticisms to which sundry accepted doctrines are subjected by the younger men to-day, in the detailed restatement of historical events which we get from modern research as our fathers could never have them--but the work itself, the complete Encyclopaedia or Dictionary of Ignorance and Error, will never be printed. It is a great pity.

Incidentally one may remark that the process by which a particular error is propagated is as interesting to watch as the way in which a plant grows.

The first step seems to be the establishing of an authority and the giving of that authority a name which comes to connote doctrinal infallibility. A very good example of this is the title "Science." Mere physical research, its achievements, its certitudes, even its conflicting and self-contradictory hypotheses, having got lumped together in many minds under this one title Science, the title is now sacred. It is used as a priestly title, as an immediate estopper to doubt or criticism.

The next step is a very interesting one for the student of psychical pathology to note. It seems to be a disease as native and universal to the human mind as is the decay of the teeth to the human body. It seems as though we all must suffer somewhat from it, and most of us suffer a great deal from it, though in a cool aspect we easily perceive it to be a lesion of thought. And this second step is as follows:

The whole lump having been given its sacred title and erected into an infallible authority, which you are to accept as directly superior to yourself and all personal sources of information, there is attributed to this idol a number of attributes. We give it a soul, and a habit and manners which do not attach to its stuff at all. The projection of this imagined living character in our authority is comparable to what we also do with mountains, statues, towns, and so forth. Our living individuality lends individuality to them. I might here digress to discuss whether this habit of the mind were not a distorted reflection of some truth, and whether, indeed, there be not such beings as demons or the souls of things. But, to leave that, we take our authority--this thing "Science," for instance--we clothe it with a creed and appetites and a will, and all the other human attributes.

This done, we set out in the third step in our progress towards fixed error. We make the idol speak. Of course, being only an idol, it talks nonsense. But by the previous steps just referred to we must believe that nonsense, and believe it we do. Thus it is, I think, that fixed error is most generally established.

I have already given one example in the hierarchic title "Science."

It was but the other day that I picked up a weekly paper in which a gentleman was discussing ghosts--that is, the supposed apparition of the living and the dead: of the dead though dead, and of the living though absent.

Nothing has been more keenly discussed since the beginning of human discussions. Are these phenomena (which undoubtedly happen) what modern people call subjective, or are they what modern people call objective? In old-fashioned English, Are the ghosts really there or are they not? The most elementary use of the human reason persuades us that the matter is not susceptible of positive proof. The criterion of certitude in any matter of perception is an inner sense in the perceiver that the thing he perceives is external to himself. He is the only witness; no one can corroborate or dispute him. The seer may be right or he may be wrong, but we have no proof--and only according to our temperament, our fancy, our experience, our mood, do we decide with one or the other of the two great schools.

Well, the gentleman of whom I am speaking wrote and had printed in plain English this phrase (read it carefully):--"Science teaches us that these phenomena are purely subjective."

Now I am quite sure that of the thousands who read that phrase all but a handful read it in the spirit in which one hears the oracle of a god. Some read it with regret, some with pleasure, but all with acquiescence.

That physical science was not competent in the matter one way or the other each of those readers would probably have discovered, if even so simple a corrective as the use of the term "physical research" instead of the sacred term "science" had been applied; the hierarchic title "Science" did the trick.

I might take another example out of many hundreds to show what I mean. You have an authority which is called, where documents are concerned, "The Best Modern Criticism." "The Best Modern Criticism" decides that "Tam o' Shanter" was written by a committee of permanent officials of the Board of Trade, or that Napoleon Bonaparte never existed. As a matter of fact, the tomfoolery does not usually venture upon ground so near home, but it talks rubbish just as monstrous about a poem a few hundred or a few thousand years old, or a great personality a few hundred or a few thousand years old.

Now if you will look at that phrase "The Best Modern Criticism" you will see at once that it simply teems with assumption and tautology. But it does more and worse: it presupposes that an infallible authority must of its own nature be perpetually wrong.

Even supposing that I have the most "modern" (that is, merely the latest) criticism to hand, and even supposing that by some omniscience of mine I can tell which is "the best" (that is, which part of it has really proved most ample, most painstaking, most general, and most sincere), even then the phrase fatally condemns me. It is to say that Wednesday is always infallible as compared with Tuesday, and Thursday as compared with Wednesday, which is absurd.

The B.M.C. tells me in 1875 that the Song of Roland could have no origins anterior to the year 1030. But the B.M.C. of 1885 (being a B.M.C. and nothing more valuable) has a changed opinion. It must change its opinion, that is the law of its being, since an integral factor in its value is its modernity. In 1885 B.M.C. tells me that the Song of Roland can be traced to origins far earlier, let us say to 912.

In 1895 B.M.C. has come to other conclusions--the Song of Roland is certainly as late as 1115 ... and so forth.

Now you would say that an idol of that absurdity could have no effect upon sane men. Change the terms and give it another name, and you would laugh at the idea of its having an effect upon any men. But we know as a matter of fact that it commands the thoughts of nearly all men to-day and makes cowards of the most learned.

Perhaps you will ask me at the end of so long a criticism in what way error may be corrected, since there is this sort of tendency in us to accept it, to which I answer that things correct it, or as the philosophers call things, "Reality." Error does not wash.

To go back to that example of ghosts. If ever you see a ghost (my poor reader), I shall ask you afterwards whether he seemed subjective or no. I think you will find the word "subjective" an astonishingly thin one--if, at least, I catch you early after the experience.

The Great Sight

All night we had slept on straw in a high barn. The wood of its beams was very old, and the tiles upon the roof were green with age; but there hung from beam to beam, fantastically, a wire caught by nails, and here and there from this wire hung an electric-light bulb. It was a symbol of the time, and the place, and the people. There was no local by-law to forbid such a thing, or if there was, no one dreamt of obeying it.

Just in the first dawn of that September day we went out, my companion and I, at guesswork to hunt in the most amusing kind of hunting, which is the hunting of an army. The lane led through one of those lovely ravines of Picardy which travellers never know (for they only see the plains), and in a little while we thought it wise to strike up the steep bank from the valley on to the bare plateau above, but it was all at random and all guesswork, only we wisely thought that we were nearing the beginning of things, and that on the bare fields of the high flat we should have a greater horizon and a better chance of catching any indications of men or arms.

When we had reached the height the sun had long risen, but it as yet gave no shining and there were no shadows, for a delicate mist hung all about the landscape, though immediately above us the sky was faintly blue.

It was the weirdest of sensations to go for mile after mile over that vast plain, to know that it was cut in regular series by parallel ravines which in all that extended view we could not guess at; to see up to the limits of the plateau the spires of villages and the groups of trees about them, and to know that somewhere in all this there lay concealed a corps d'armée--and not to see or hear a soul. The only human being that we saw was a man driving a heavy farm cart very slowly up a side-way just as we came into the great road which has shot dead across this country in one line ever since the Romans built it. As we went along that road, leaving the fields, we passed by many men indeed, and many houses, all in movement with the early morning; and the chalked numbers on the doors, and here and there an empty tin of polishing-paste or an order scrawled on paper and tacked to a wall betrayed the passage of soldiers. But of the army there was nothing at all. Scouting on foot (for that was what it was) is a desperate business, and that especially if you have nothing to tell you whether you will get in touch in five, or ten, or twenty miles.

It was nine o'clock before a clatter of horse-hoofs came up the road behind us. At first my companion and I wondered whether it were the first riders of the Dragoons or Cuirassiers. In that case the advance was from behind us. But very soon, as the sound grew clearer, we heard how few they were, and then there came into view, trotting rapidly, a small escort and two officers with the umpires' badges, so there was nothing doing; but when, half a mile ahead of us on the road, they turned off to the left over plough, we knew that that was the way we must follow too. Before we came to the turning-place, before we left the road to take the fields on the left, there came from far off and on our right the sound of a gun.

It was my companion who heard it first. We strained to hear it again; twice we thought we had caught it, and then again twice we doubted. It is not so easily recognizable a sound as you might think in those great plains cut by islands of high trees and steading walls. The little "75" gun lying low makes a different sound altogether at a distance from the old piece of "90." At any rate there was here no doubt that there were guns to the right and in front of us, and the umpire had gone to the left. We were getting towards the thick, and we had only to go straight on to find out where the front was.

Just as we had so decided and were still pursuing the high road, there came, not half a mile away and again to our right, in a valley below us, that curious sound which is like nothing at all unless it be dumping of flints out of a cart: rifle fire. It cracked and tore in stretches. Then there were little gaps of silence like the gaps in signalling, and then it cracked and tore in stretches again; and then, fitfully, one individual shot and then another would be heard; and, much further off, with little sounds like snaps, the replies began from the hillside beyond the stream. So far so good. Here was contact in the valley below us, and the guns, some way behind and far off northwards, had opened. So we got the hang of it instantly-- the front was a sort of a crescent lying roughly north and south, and roughly parallel to the great road, and the real or feigned mass of the advance was on the extreme left of that front. We were in it now, and that anxious and wearing business in all hunting, finding, was over; but we had been on foot six mortal hours before coming across our luck, and more than half the soldiers' day was over. These men had been afoot since three, and certain units on the left had already marched over twenty miles.

After that coming in touch with our business, not only did everything become plain, but the numbers we met, and what I have called "the thick of things," fed us with interest. We passed half the 38th, going down the road singing, to extend the line, and in a large village we came to the other half, slouching about in the traditional fashion of the Service; they had been waiting for an hour. With them, and lined up all along the village street, was one battery, with the drivers dismounted, and all that body were at ease. There were men sitting on the doorsteps of the houses and men trotting to the canteen-wagon or to the village shops to buy food; and there were men reading papers which a pedlar had brought round. Mud and dust had splashed them all; upon some there was a look of great fatigue; they were of all shapes and sizes, and altogether it was the sort of sight you would not see in any other service in the world. It was the sort of sight which so disgusted the Emperor Joseph when he made his little tour to spy out the land before the Revolutionary Wars. It was the sort of sight which made Massenbach before Grandpré marvel whether the French forces were soldiers at all, and the sort of sight which made Valmy inexplicable to the King of Prussia and his staff. It was the sort of sight which eighteen months later still convinced Mack in Tournai that the Duke of York's plan was a plan "of annihilation." It is a trap for judgment is the French service.

So they lounged about and bought bread, and shifted their packs, and so the drivers stood by their horses, and so they all waited and slouched; until there came, not a man with a bugle nor anything with the slightest savour of drama but a little fellow running along thumping in his loose leather leggings, who went up to a Major of Artillery and saluted, and immediately afterwards the Major put his hand up, and then down a village street, from a point which we could not see came a whistle, and the whole of that mass of men began to swarm. The grey-blue coats of the line swung round the corner of the village street; they had yet a few miles before them. Anything more rapid or less in step it would be difficult to conceive. The guns were off at a right angle down the main road, making a prodigious clatter, and at the same time appeared two parties, one of which it was easy to understand, the other not. They were both parties of sappers. The one party had a great roll of wire on a drum, and as quick as you could think they were unreeling it, and as they unreeled it fastening it to eaves, overhanging branches, and to corners of walls, stretching it out forward. It was the field-telephone. The other party came along carrying great beams upon their shoulders, but what they were to do with these beams we did not know.

We followed the tail of the line down into the valley, and all that morning long and past the food time at midday, and so till the sun declined in the afternoon, we went with the 38th in its gradual success from crest to crest. And still the 38th slouched by companies, and mile after mile with checks and halts, and it never seemed to get either less or more tired. The men had had twelve

119

hours of it when they came at last, and we after them, on to the critical position. They had carried (together with all the line to left and to the right of them) a string of villages which crowned the crest of a further plateau, and over this further plateau they were advancing against the main body of the resistance--the other army corps which was set up against ours, to simulate an enemy.

A railway line ran here across the rolling hedgeless fields, and just at the point where my companion and I struck it there was a dip in the land and a high embankment which hid the plain beyond; but from that plain beyond one heard the separate fire of the advancing line in its scattered order. We climbed the embankment, and from its ridge we saw over two miles or more of stubble, the little creeping bunches of the attack. What was resisting, or where it lay, one could only guess. Some hundreds of yards before us to the east, with the sloping sun full on it, a line of thicket, one scattered wood and then another, an imperceptible lifting of the earth here and there marked the opposing firing line. Two pompoms could be spotted exactly, for the flashes were clear through the underwood. And still the tide of the advance continued to flow, and the little groups came up and fed it, one after another and another, in the centre where we were, and far away to the north and right away to the south the countryside was alive with it. The action was beginning to take on something of that final movement and decision which makes the climax of manoeuvres look so great a game. But in a little while that general creeping forward was checked: there were orders coming from the umpires, and a sort of lull fell over each position held. My companion said to me:

"Let us go forward now over the intervening zone and in among Picquart's men, and get well behind their line, and see whether there is a rally or whether before the end of this day they begin to fall back again."

So we did, walking a mile or so until we had long passed their outposts and were behind their forward lines. And standing there, upon a little eminence near a wood, we turned and looked over what we had come, westward towards the sun which was now not far from its setting. Then it was that we saw the last of the Great Sight.

The level light, mellow and already reddening, illumined all that plain strangely, and with the absolute stillness of the air contrasted the opening of the guns which had been brought up to support the renewal of the attack. We saw the isolated woods standing up like islands with low steep cliffs, dotted in a sea of stubble for miles and miles, and first from the cover of one and then from another the advance perpetually, piercing and deploying. As we so watched there buzzed high above us, like a great hornet, a biplane, circling well within our lines, beyond attack from the advance, but overlooking all they concealed behind it. In a few minutes a great Bleriot monoplane like a hawk followed, yet further inwards. The two great birds shot round in an arc, parallel to the firing line, and well behind it, and in a few minutes, that seemed seconds, they were dots to the south and then lost in the air. And perpetually, as the sun declined, Picquart's men were falling back north and south of us and before us, and the advance continued. Group by group we saw it piercing this hedge, that woodland, now occupying a nearer and a nearer roll of land. It was the greatest thing imaginable: this enormous sweep of men, the dead silence of the air, and the comparatively slight contrast of the ceaseless pattering rifle fire and the slight intermittent accompaniment of the advancing batteries; until the sun set and all this human business slackened. Then for the first time one heard bugles, which were a command to cease the game.

I would not have missed that day nor lose the memories of it for anything in the world.

The Decline of a State

The decline of a State is not equivalent to a mortal sickness therein. States are organisms subject to diseases and to decay as are the organisms of men's bodies; but they are not subject to a rhythmic rise and fall as is the body of a man. A State in its decline is never a State doomed or a State dying. States perish slowly or by violence, but never without remedy and rarely without violence.

The decline of a State differs with the texture of it. A democratic State will decline from a lowering of its potential, that is of its ever-ready energy to act in a crisis, to correct and to control its servants in common times, to watch them narrowly and suspect them at all times. A despotic State will decline when the despot is not in point of fact the true depository of despotic power, but some other acting in his name, of whom the people know little and cannot judge; or when the despot, though fully in view and recognized, lacks will; or when (which is rare) he is so inhuman as to miss the general sense of his subjects. An oligarchic State, or aristocracy as it is called, will decline principally through two agencies which are, first, illusion, and secondly, lack of civic aptitude. For an oligarchic State tends very readily to illusion, being conducted by men who live at leisure, satisfy their passions, are immune from the laws, and prefer to shield themselves from reality. Their capacity or appetite for illusion will rapidly pervade those below them, for in an aristocracy the rulers are subjected to a sort of worship from the rest of the community, and thus it comes about that aristocracies in their decline accept fantastic histories of their own past, conceive victory possible without armies, wealth to be an indication of ability, and national security to be a natural gift rather than a product of the will. Such communities further fail from the lack of civic aptitude, as was said above, which means that they deliberately elect to leave the mass of citizens incompetent and irresponsible for generations, so that, when any more strain is upon them, they look at once for some men other than themselves to relieve them, and are incapable of corporate action upon their own account.

The decline of a State differs also according to whether it be a great State or a small one, for in the first indifference, in the latter faction, are a peril, and in the first ignorance, in the latter private spite.

Then again, the decline of a State will differ according to whether its strength is rooted originally in commerce, in arms, or in production; and if in production, then whether in the production of the artisan or in that of the peasant. If arms be the basis of the State, then that the army should become professional and apart is a symptom of decline and a cause of it; if commerce, the substitution of hazards and imaginaries for the transport of real goods and the search after real demand; if production, the discontent or apathy of the producer; as with peasants an ill system in the taxation of the land or in the things necessary for its tillage, such as a misgovernment of its irrigation in a dry country; the permission of private exactions and tolls in a fertile one; the toleration of thieves and forestallers, and so forth. Artisans, upon the other hand, may well flourish, though the State be corrupt in such matters, but they must be secured in a high wage and be given a vast liberty of protest, for if they sink to be slaves in fact, they will from the nature of their toil grow both weak and foolish. Yet is not the State endangered by the artisan's throwing off a refuse of ill-paid and starving men who are either too many for the work or unskilful at it? Such an excretion would poison a peasantry, remaining in their body as it were, but artisans are purged thereby. This refuse it is for the State to decide upon. It may in an artisan State be used for soldiery (since such States commonly maintain but small armies and are commonly indifferent to military glory), or it may be set to useful labour, or again, destroyed; but this last use is repugnant to humanity, and so in the long run hurtful to the State.

In the decline of a State, of whatever nature that State be, two vices will immediately appear and grow: these are Avarice and Fear; and men will more readily accept the imputation of Avarice than of Fear, for Avarice is the less despicable of the two--yet in fact Fear will be by far the strongest passion of the time.

Avarice will show itself not indeed in a mere greed of gain (for this is common to all societies whether flourishing or failing), but rather in a sort of taking for granted and permeation of the mere love of money, so that history will be explained by it, wars judged by their booty or begun in order to enrich a few, love between men and women wholly subordinated to it, especially among the rich: wealth made a test for responsibility and great salaries invented and paid to those who serve the State. This vice will also be apparent in the easy acquaintance of all who are possessed of wealth and their segregation from the less fortunate, for avarice cleaves society flatways, keeping the scum of it quite clear of the middle, the middle of it quite clear of the dregs, and so forth. It is a further mark of avarice in its last stages that the rich are surrounded with lies in which they themselves believe. Thus, in the last phase, there are no parasites but only friends, no gifts but only loans, which are more esteemed favours than gifts once were. No one vicious but only tedious, and no one a poltroon but only slack.

Of Fear in the decline of a State it may be said that it is so much the master passion of such decline as to eat up all others. Coming by travel from a healthy State to one diseased, Fear is the first point you take. Men dare not print or say what they feel of the judges, the public governors, the action of the police, the controllers of fortunes and of news. This Fear will have about it something comic, providing infinite joy to the foreigner, and modifying with laughter the lament of the patriot. A miserable hack that never had a will of his own, but ran to do what he was told for twenty years at the bidding of his masters, being raised to the Bench will be praised for an impartial virtue more than human. A drunken fellow, the son of a drunkard, having stolen control over some half-dozen sheets, must be named under the breath or not at all. A powerful minister may be accused with sturdy courage of something which he did not do and no one would mind his doing, but under the influence of Fear, to tell the least little truth about him will put a whole assembly into a sort of blankness.

This vice has for its most laughable effect the raising of a whole host of phantoms, and when a State is so far gone that civic Fear is quite normal to the citizens, then you will find them blenching with terror at a piece of print, a whispered accusation. Bankruptcy, though they be possessed of nothing, and even the ill-will of women. Moneylenders under this influence have the greatest power, next after them, blackmailers of all kinds, and next after these eccentrics who may blurt or break out. Those who have least power in the decline of a State, are priests, soldiers, the mothers of many children, the lovers of one woman, and saints.

On Past Greatness

There lies in the North-East of France, close against the Belgian frontier and within cannon shot of the famous battlefield of Malplaquet, a little town called Bavai--I have written of it elsewhere.

Coming into this little town you seem to be entering no more than a decent, unimportant market borough, a larger village meant for country folk, perhaps without a history and certainly without fame.

As you come to look about you one thing after another enlivens your curiosity and suggests something at once enormous and remote in the destinies of the place.

In the first place, seven great roads go out like the seven rays of a star, plumb straight, darting along the line, across the vast, bare fields of Flanders, past and along the many isolated woods of the provinces, and making to great capitals far off--to Cologne, to Paris, to Treves, and to the ports of the sea.

These roads are deserted in great part. Some of them are metalled in certain sections, and again in other sections are no more than lanes, and again no more than footpaths, as you proceed along their miles of way; but their exact design awfully impresses the mind. You know, as you follow such strict alignment, that you are fulfilling the majestic purpose of Imperial Rome. It was the Romans that made these things.

Then, intrigued and excited by such remains of greatness, you read what you can of the place.... And you find nothing but a dust of legend. You find a story that once here a king, filled with ambition and worshipping strange gods, thrust out these great roads to the ends of the earth; desired his capital to be a hub and navel for the world. He put them under the protection of the seven planets and of the deities of those stars. Three he paved with black marble and four with white marble, and where they met upon the market place he put up a golden terminal. There the legend ends.

It is only legend--a true product of the Dark Ages, when all that Rome had done rose like a huge dream in the mind of Europe and took on gorgeous and fantastic colouring. You learn (for the rest) very little--that ornaments and money have been found dating from two thousand years, that once great walls surrounded the place. It must have had noble buildings and solemn courts. In strict history all you will discover is that it was the capital of that tribe, the Nervii, against whom Caesar fought, and whose territory was early conquered for the Empire. You will find nothing more. There is no living tradition, there is no voice; the little town is dumb.

The place is a figure, and a striking one, of greatness long dead, and a man visiting its small domestic interests to-day, and noting its comfort, its humility, and its sleep, is reminded of many things attaching to human fame. It would seem as though the ambitions of men, and that exalted appetite for glory which has produced the chief things of this world, suffer the effect of time somewhat as the body of an animal slain will suffer that.

One part of the organism and then another decays and mixes back with nature. The effect of will has vanished. The thing is a prey to all that environment which, once alive, it combated, conquered, and transformed to its own use. One portion after another is lost, until at last only the most resisting stands--the skeleton and hard framework, the least expressive, the least personal part of the whole. This also decays and perishes. Then there remains no more but a score of hardened fragments that linger in their place, and what has passed away is fortunate if even the slightest or most fantastic legend of itself survives.

The great dead are first forgotten in their physical habit; we lose the nature of their voices, we forget their sympathies and their affections. Bit by bit all that they intended to be eternal slips back into the common thing around. A blurred image, growing fainter and fainter, lingers. At last the person vanishes, and in its place some public raising material things--a monument, a tomb, an ornament, or weapon of enduring metal--is all that remains.

If it were possible for the spring of appetite and quest to be dried up in man, such a spectacle would dry up that spring.

It is not possible, for it is providentially in the nature of man to cherish these illusions of an immortal memory and of a life bestowed upon the shade or the mere name of his living greatness. Those various forms of fame which are young men's goals, and to which the eager creative power of early manhood so properly directs itself, seem each in turn or each for its varying temperament to promise the desired reward; and one imagines that his love, another that his discoveries, another that his victories in the field or his conspicuous acts of courage will remain permanently with his fellows long after he has left their feast.

As though to give some substance to the flattering cheat, there is one kind of fame which men have been permitted to attain, and which does give them a sort of fixed tenure--if not for ever, yet for generations upon generations--in the human city. This sort of fame is the fame of the great poets. There is nothing more enduring. It has for some who were most blessed outlasted, you may say, all material things which they handled or they knew--all fabrics, all instruments, all habitations. It is comparable in its endurance to the years, and a man reads the "Song of Roland" and can still look on that same unchanged Cleft of Roncesvalles, or a man reads the Iliad and can look to-day westward from the shores to Tenedos. But wait a moment. Are they indeed blessed in this, the great poets? Ronsard debated it. He decided that they were, and put into the mouth of the muses the great lines:----

> Mais un tel accident n'arrive point a l'âme,
> Qui sans matière vist immortelle là haut.
>
> Vela saigement dit, Ceux dont la fantaisie
> Sera religieuse et devote envers Dieu
> Tousjours acheveront quelque grand poésie,
> Et dessus leur renom la Parque n'aura lieu.

But the matter is still undecided.

Mr. The Duke

The Man of Malplaquet

On the field of Malplaquet, that battlefield, I met a man.

He was pointed out to me as a man who drove travellers to Bavai. His name was Mr. The Duke, and he was very poor.

If he comes across these lines (which is exceedingly unlikely) I offer him my apologies. Anyhow, I can write about him freely, for he is not rich, and, what is more, the laws of his country permit the telling of the truth about our fellow-men, even when they are rich.

Mr. The Duke was of some years, and his colour was that of cedar wood. I met him in his farmyard, and I said to him:

"Is it you, sir, that drive travellers to Bavai?"

"No," said he.

Accustomed by many years of travel to this type of response, I continued:

"How much do you charge?"

"Two francs fifty," said he.

"I will give you three francs," I said, and when I had said this he shook his head and replied:

"You fall at an evil moment; I was about to milk the cows." Having said this he went to harness the horse.

When the horse was harnessed to his little cart (it was an extremely small horse, full of little bones and white in colour, with one eye stronger than the other) he gave it to his little daughter to hold, and himself sat down to table, proposing a meal.

"It is but humble fare," he said, "for we are poor."

This sounded familiar to me; I had both read and heard it before. The meal was of bread and butter, pasty and beer, for Malplaquet is a country of beer and not of wine.

As he sat at table the old man pointed out to me that contraband across the Belgian frontier, which is close by, was no longer profitable.

"The Fraud," he said, "is no longer a living for anyone."

Upon that frontier contraband is called "The Fraud"; it holds an honourable place as a career.

"The Fraud," he continued, "has gone long ago; it has burst. It is no longer to be pursued. There is not even any duty upon apples.... But there is a duty upon pears. Had I a son I would not put him into The Fraud.... Sometimes there is just a chance here and there.... One can pick up an occasion. But take it all in all (and here he wagged his head solemnly) there is nothing in it any more."

I said that I had no experience of contraband professionally, but that I knew a very honest man who lived by it in the country of Andorra, and that according to my morals a man had a perfect right to run the risk and take his chance, for there was no contract between him and the power he was trying to get round. This announcement pleased the old gentleman, but it did not grip his mind. He was of your practical sort. He was almost a Pragmatist. Abstractions wearied him. He put no faith in the reality of ideas. I think he was a Nominalist like Abelard: and whatever excuse you may make for him, Abelard was a Nominalist right enough, for it was the intellectual thing to be at the time, though St. Bernard utterly confuted him in arguments of enormous length and incalculable boredom.

The old man, then, I say, would have nothing to do with first principles, and he reasserted his position that, in the concrete, in the existent world, The Fraud no longer paid.

This said for the sixth or seventh time, he drank some brandy to put heart into him and climbed up into his little cart, I by his side. He hit the white horse with a stick, making at the same time an extraordinary shrill noise with his mouth, like a siren, and the horse began to slop and sludge very dolefully towards Bavai.

"This horse," said Mr. The Duke, "is a wonderfully good horse. He goes like the wind. He is of Arab extraction, and comes from Africa."

With these words he gave the horse another huge blow with his stick, and once more emitted his piercing cry. The horse went neither faster nor slower than before, and seemed very indifferent to the whole performance.

"He is from Africa," said Mr. The Duke again, meditatively. "Do you know Africa?"

Africa with the French populace means Algiers. I answered that I knew it, and that in particular I knew the road southward from Constantine. At this he looked very pleased, and said:

"I was a soldier in Africa. I deserted seven times."

To this I made no answer. I did not know how he wanted me to take it, so I waited until he should speak again, which he soon did, and said:

"The last time I deserted I was free for a year and a half. I used to conduct beasts; that was my trade. When they caught me I was to have been shot. I was saved by the tears of a woman!"

Having said this the old man pulled out a very small pipe and

129

filled it with exceedingly black tobacco. He lit it, then he began talking again rather more excitedly.

"It is a terrible thing and an unhappy thing none the less," he went on, "that a man should be taken out to be shot and should be saved by the tears of a woman." Then he added, "Of what use are wars? How foolish it is that men should kill each other! If there were a war I would not fight. Would you?"

I said I thought I would; but whether I should like to or not would depend upon the war.

He was eager to contradict and to tell me that war was wrong and stupid. Having behind him the logical training of fifteen Christian centuries he was in no way muddle-headed upon the matter. He saw very well that his doctrine meant that it was wrong to have a country, and wrong to love it, and that patriotism was all bosh, and that no ideal was worth physical pain or trouble. To such conclusions had he come at the end of his life.

The white horse meanwhile slouched; Bavai grew somewhat nearer as we sat in silence after his last sentence. He was turning many things over in his mind. He veered off on to political economy.

"When the rich man at the Manufactory here, the place where they sell phosphates for the land, when he stands beer to all the workmen and to the countryside, I always say, 'Fools! All this will be put on to the cost of the phosphates; they will cost you more!'"

Mr. The Duke did not accept John Stuart Mill's proposition upon the cost of production nor the general theories of Ricardo upon which Mill's propositions were based. In his opinion rent was a factor in the cost of production, for he told me that butter had gone up because the price of land was rising near the towns. In what he next said I found out that he was not a Collectivist, for he said a man should own enough to live upon, but he said that this was impossible if rich people were allowed to live. I asked him what the politics of the countryside were and how people voted. He said:

"The politicians trick the people. They are a heap of worthlessness."

I asked him if he voted, and he said "yes." He said there was only one way to vote, but I did not understand what this meant.

Had time served I should have asked him further questions-- upon the nature of the soul, its ultimate fate, the origin of man and his destiny, whether mortal or immortal; the proper constitution of the State, the choice of the legislator, the prince, and the magistrate; the function of art, whether it is subsidiary or primary in human life; the family; marriage. Upon the State he had already informed me, and also upon the institution of property, and upon his view of armies. Upon all those other things he would equally have given me

130

a clear reply, for he was a man that knew his own mind, and that is more than most people can say.

But we were now in Bavai, and I had no time to discover more. We drank together before we parted, and I was very pleased to see the honest look in his face. With more leisure and born to greater opportunities he would have been talked about, this Man of Malplaquet. He had come to his odd conclusions as the funny people do in Scandinavia and in Russia, and among the rich intellectuals and usurers in London and Berlin; but he was a jollier man than they are, for he could drive a horse and lie about it, and he could also milk a cow. As we parted he used a phrase that wounded me, and which I had only heard once before in my life. He said:

"We shall never see each other again!"

Another man had once said this thing to me before. This man was a farmer in the Northumbrian hills, who walked with me a little way in the days when I was going over Carter Fell to find the Scots people, many, many years ago. He also said: "We shall never meet again!"

The Game of Cards

A youth of no more than twenty-three years entered a first-class carriage at the famous station of Swindon in the county of Wiltshire, proposing to travel to the uttermost parts of the West and to enjoy a comfortable loneliness while he ruminated upon all things human and divine; when he was sufficiently annoyed to discover that in the further corner of the carriage was sitting an old gentleman of benevolent appearance, or at any rate a gentleman of benevolent appearance who appeared in his youthful eyes to be old.

For though the old gentleman was, as a fact, but sixty, yet his virile beard had long gone white and the fringes of hair attaching to his ostrich egg of a head confirmed his venerable appearance.

When the train had started the young man proceeded in no very good temper and with great solemnity to fill a pipe. He turned to his senior, who was watching him in a very paternal and happy manner, and said formally:

"I hope you do not mind my smoking, sir?"

"Not at all," said the old boy; "it is a habit I have long grown accustomed to in others."

The young man bowed in a somewhat absurd fashion and felt for his matches. He discovered to his no small mortification that he had none. He was so used to his pipe after a meal that he really could not forgo it. He came off his perch by at least three steps and asked the old man very gently whether he had any matches.

The older man produced a box and at the same time brought out with it a little notebook and a playing card which happened to be in his pocket. The young man took the matches and lit his pipe, surveying the old man the while with a more complacent eye.

"It is very kind of you, sir," he said a little less stiffly. He handed back the matches, wrapped his rug round his legs, sat down in his place, and knowing that one should prolong the conversation for a moment or two after a favour, said: "I see that you play cards."

"I do," said the old man simply; "would you like a game?"

"I don't mind," said the young man, who had always heard that it was unmanly and ridiculous to refuse a game of cards in a railway carriage.

The elder man laughed merrily in his strong beard as he saw his junior begin to spread somewhat awkwardly a copy of a newspaper upon his knees. "I'll show you a trick worth two of that," he said, and taking one of the first-class cushions, which alone of railway cushions are movable from its place, he came over to the

132

corner opposite the young man and made a table of the cushion between them. "Now," said he genially, "what's it to be?"

"Well," said the young man like one who expounds new mysteries, "do you know piquet?"

"Oh, yes," said his companion with another happy little laugh of contentment with the world. "I'll take you on. What shall it be?"

"Pennies if you like," said the young man nonchalantly.

"Very well, and double for the Rubicon."

"How do you mean?" said the young man, puzzled.

"You will see," said the old man, and they began to play.

The game was singularly absorbing. At first the young man won a few pounds; then he lost rather heavily, then he won again, but not quite enough to recoup. Then in the fourth game he won, so that he was a little ahead, and meanwhile the old man chatted merrily during the discarding or the shuffling: during the shuffling especially. He looked out towards the downs with something of a sigh at one moment, and said:

"It's a happy world."

"Yes," answered the younger man with the proper lugubriousness of youth, "but it all comes to an end."

"It isn't its coming to an end," said the elder man, declaring a point of six, "that's not the tragedy; it's the little bits coming to an end meanwhile, before the whole comes to an end: that's the tragedy...." But he added with another of his jolly laughs: "We must play. Piquet takes up all one's grey matter."

They played and the young man lost again, but by a very narrow margin: it was quite an absorbing game. As they shuffled again the young man said:

"What did you mean by the little bits stopping, or whatever it was?"

"Oh," said the old man as though he couldn't remember, and then he added: "Oh, yes, I mean you'll find, as you grow older, people die and affections change, and, though it seems silly to mention it in company with higher things, there's what Shelley called the 'contagion of the world's slow stain.'"

Then their conversation was interrupted by the ardour of the game; but as they played the young man was ruminating, and he had come to the conclusion that his senior was imperfectly educated and was probably of the middle classes, whereas he himself was destined to be a naval architect, and with that object had recently left the university for an office in the city. The young man thought that a man properly educated would never quote a tag: he was wrong there. As he had allowed his thoughts to wander somewhat the young man lost that game rather heavily, and at the end of it he

133

was altogether about ten shillings to the bad. It was his turn to shuffle. The older man was at leisure to speak, and did so rather dreamily as he gazed at the landscape again.

"Things change, you know," he said, "and there is the contagion of the world's slow stain. One gets preoccupied: especially about money. When men marry they get very much preoccupied upon that point. It's bad for them, but it can't be helped."

"You cut," said the young man.

His elder cut and they played again. This time as they played their game the old man broke his rule of silence and continued his observations interruptedly:

"Four kings," he said.... "It isn't that a man gets to think money all-important, it is that he has to think of it all the time.... No, three queens are no good. I said four kings.... four knaves.... The little losses of money don't affect one, but perpetual trouble about it does, and" (closing up the majority of tricks which he had just gained) "many a man goes on making more year after year and yet feels himself in peril.... And the last trick." He took up the cards to shuffle them. "Towards the very end of life," he continued, "it gets less, I suppose, but you'll feel the burden of it." He put the pack over for the younger man to cut. When that was done he dealt them out slowly. As he dealt he said: "One feels the loss of little material things: objects to which one was attached, a walking-stick, or a ring, or a watch which one has carried for years. Your declare."

The young man declared, and that game was played in silence. I regret to say that the young man was Rubiconed, and was thirty shillings in the elder's debt.

"We'll stop if you like" said the elder man kindly.

"Oh, no," said the youth with nonchalance, "I'll pay you now if you like."

"Not at all, I didn't mean that," said the older man with a sudden prick of honour.

"Oh, but I will, and we'll start fair again," said the young man. Whereupon he handed over his combined losses in gold, the older man gave him change, they shuffled again, and they went on with their play.

"After all," said the older man, musing as he confessed to a point of no more than five, "it's all in the day's work.... It's just a day's work," he repeated with a saddened look in his eyes, "it's a game that one plays like this game, and then when it's over it's over. It's the little losses that count."

That game again was unfortunate for the young man, and he had to shell out fifteen and six. But the brakes were applied, Bristol was reached, the train came to a standstill, and the young man, looking up a little confused and hurried, said: "Hello, Bristol! I get out here."

"So do I," said the older man. They both stood up together, and the jolt of the train as it stopped dead threw them into each other's arms.

"I am really very sorry," said the youth.

"It's my fault," said the old chap like a good fellow, "I ought to have caught hold. You get out and I'll hand you your bag."

"It's very kind of you," said the young man. He was really flattered by so much attention, but he knew himself what a good companion he was and he could understand it; besides which they had made friends during that little journey. He always liked a man to whom he had lost some money in an honest game.

There was a heavy crowd upon the platform, and two men barging up out of it saluted the old man boisterously by the name of Jack. He twinkled at them with his eyes as he began moving the luggage about, and stood for a moment in the doorway with his own bag in his right hand and the young man's bag in his left. The young man so saw it for an instant, a fine upstanding figure--he saw his bag handed by some mistake to the second of the old man's friends, a porter came by at the moment pushing through the crowd with a trolley, an old lady made a scene, the porter apologized, the crowd took sides, some for the porter, some for the old lady; the young man, with the deference of his age, politely asked several people to make way, but when he had emerged from the struggle his companion, his companion's friends, and his own bag could not be found; or at any rate he could not make out where they were in the great mass that pushed and surged upon the platform.

He made himself a little conspicuous by asking too many questions and by losing his temper twice with people who had done him no harm, when, just as his excitement was growing more than querulous, a very heavy, stupid-looking man in regulation boots tapped him on the shoulder and said: "Follow me." He was prepared with an oath by way of reply, but another gentleman of equal weight, wearing boots of the same pattern, linked his arm in his and between them they marched him away, to a little private closet opening out of the stationmaster's room.

"Now, sir," said he who had first tapped him on the shoulder, "be good enough to explain your movements."

"I don't know what you mean," said the young man.

"You were in the company," said the older man severely, "of an old man, bald, with a white beard and a blue sailor suit. He had come from London; you joined him at Swindon. We have evidence

135

that he was to be met at this station and it will be to your advantage if you make a clean breast of it."

The young man was violent and he was borne away.

But he had friends at Bristol. He gave his references and he was released. To this day he believes that he suffered not from folly, but from injustice. He did not see his bag again, but after all it contained no more than his evening clothes, for which he had paid or rather owed six guineas, four shirts, as many collars and dress ties, a silver-mounted set of brushes and combs, and useless cut-glass bottles, a patented razor, a stick of shaving soap, and two very, very confidential letters which he treasured. His watch, of course, was gone, but not, I am glad to say, his chain, which hung dangling, though in his flurry he had not noticed it. It made him look a trifle ridiculous. As he wore no tie-pin he had not lost that, and beyond his temper he had indeed lost nothing further save, possibly, a textbook upon Thermodynamics. This book he thought he remembered having put into the bag, and if he had it belonged to his library, but he could not quite remember this point, and when the Library claimed it he stoutly disputed their claim.

In this dispute he was successful, but it was the only profit he made out of that journey, unless we are to count his experience, and experience, as all the world knows, is a thing that men must buy.

"King Lear"

The great unity which was built up two thousand years ago and was called Christendom in its final development split and broke in pieces. The various civilizations of its various provinces drifted apart, and it will be for the future historian to say at what moment the isolation of each from all was farthest pushed. It is certain that that point is passed.

In the task of reuniting what was broken--it is the noblest work a modern man can do--the very first mechanical act must be to explain one national soul to another. That act is not final. The nations of Europe, now so divided, still have more in common than those things by which they differ, and it is certain that when they have at last revealed to them their common origin they will return to it. They will return to it, perhaps, under the pressure of war waged by some not Christian civilization, but they will return. In the meanwhile, of those acts not final, yet of immediate necessity in the task of establishing unity, is the act of introducing one national soul to another.

Now this is best accomplished in a certain way which I will describe. You will take that part in the letters of a nation which you maturely judge most or best to reflect the full national soul, with its qualities, careless of whether these be great or little; you will take such a work as reproduces for you as you read it, not only in its sentiment, but in its very rhythm, the stuff and colour of the nation; this you will present to the foreigner, who cannot understand. His efforts must be laborious, very often unfruitful, but where it is fruitful it will be of a decisive effect.

Thus let anyone take some one of the immortal things that Racine wrote and show them to an Englishman. He will hardly ever be able to make anything of it at first. Here and there some violently emotional passage may faintly touch him, but the mass of the verse will seem to him dead. Now, if by constant reading, by association with those who know what Racine is, he at last sees him--and these changes in the mind come very suddenly--he will see into the soul of Gaul. For the converse task, to-day not equally difficult but once almost impossible, of presenting England to the French intelligence--or, indeed, to any other alien intelligence--you may choose the play "King Lear."

That play has every quality which does reflect the soul of the community in which and for which it was written. Note a few in their order.

First, it is not designed to its end; at least it is not designed accurately to its end; it is written as a play and it is meant to be acted as a play, and it is the uniform opinion of those versed in plays and in acting that in its full form it could hardly be presented, while in any form it is the hardest even of Shakespeare's plays to perform. Here you have a parallel with a thousand mighty English things to which you can turn. Is there not institution after institution to decide on, so lacking a complete fitness to its end, larger in a way than the end it is to serve, and having, as it were, a life of its own which proceeds apart from its effect? This quality which makes so many English things growths rather than instruments is most evident in the great play.

Again, it has that quality which Voltaire noted, which he thought abnormal in Shakespeare, but which is the most national characteristic in him, that a sort of formlessness, if it mars the framework of the thing and spoils it, yet also permits the exercise of an immeasurable vitality. When a man has read "King Lear" and lays down the book he is like one who has been out in one of those empty English uplands in a storm by night. It is written as though the pen bred thoughts. It is possible to conjecture as one reads, and especially in the diatribes, that the pen itself was rapid and the brain too rapid for the pen. One feels the rush of the air. Now, this quality is to be discovered in the literature of many nations, but never with the fullness which it has in the literature of England. And note that in those phases of the national life when foreign models have constrained this instinct of expansion in English verse, they never have restrained it for long, and that even through the bonds established by those models the instinct of expansion breaks. You see it in the exuberance of Dryden and in the occasional running rhetoric of Pope, until it utterly loosens itself with the end of the eighteenth century.

The play is national, again, in that permanent curiosity upon knowable things--nay, that mysterious half-knowledge of unknowable things--which, in its last forms, produced the mystic, and which is throughout history so plainly characteristic of these Northern Atlantic islands. Every play of Shakespeare builds with that material, and no writer, even of the English turn, has sent out points further into the region of what is not known than Shakespeare has in sudden flashes of phrase. But "King Lear," though it contains a lesser number of lines of this mystical and half-religious effect than, say, "Hamlet," yet as a general impression is the more mystical of the two plays. The element of madness, which in "Hamlet" hangs in the background like a storm-cloud ready to break, in "King Lear" rages; and it is the use of this which lends its amazing psychical power to the play. It has been said (with no great profundity of criticism) that English fiction is chiefly remarkable for its power of particularization of character, and that where French work, for instance, will present ideas, English will present persons. The judgment is grossly insufficient, and therefore false, but it is based upon a proof which is very salient in English letters, which is that, say, in quite short and modern work the sense of complete unity deadens the English mind. The same nerve which revolts at a straight road and at a code of law revolts against one tone of thought, and the sharp contrast of emotional character, not the dual contrast which is common to all literatures, but the multiple contrast, runs through "King Lear" and gives the work such a tone that one seems as one reads it to be moving in a cloud.

The conclusion is perhaps Shakespearean rather than English, and in a fashion escapes from any national labelling. But the note of silence which Shakespeare suddenly brings in upon the turmoil, and with which he is so fond of completing what he has done, would not be possible were not that spirit of expansion and of a kind of literary adventurousness present in all that went before.

It is indeed this that makes the play so memorable. And it may not be fantastic to repeat and expand what has been said above in other words, namely, that King Lear has something about him which seems to be a product of English landscape and of English weather, and if its general movement is a storm its element is one of those sudden silences that come sometimes with such magical rapidity after the booming of the wind.

The Excursion

It is so old a theme that I really hesitate to touch it; and yet it is so true and so useful that I will. It is true all the time, and it is particularly useful at this season of the year to men in cities: to all repetitive men: to the men that read these words. What is more, true as it is and useful as it is, no amount of hammering at people seems to get this theme into their practice; though it has long ago entered into their convictions they will not act upon it in their summers. And this true and useful theme is the theme of little freedoms and discoveries, the value of getting loose and away by a small trick when you want to get your glimpse of Fairyland.

Now how does one get loose and away?

When a man says to himself that he must have a holiday he means that he must see quite new things that are also old: he desires to open that door which stood wide like a window in childhood and is now shut fast. But where are the new things that are also the old? Paradoxical fellows who deserve drowning tell one that they are at our very doors. Well, that is true of the eager mind, but the mind is no longer eager when it is in need of a holiday. And you can get at the new things that are also the old by way of drugs, but drugs are a poor sort of holiday fabric. If you have stored up your memory well with much experience you can get these things from your memory--but only in a pale sort of way.

I think the best avenue to recreation by the magical impressions of the world upon the mind is this: To go to some place to which the common road leads you and then to get just off the common road. You will be astonished to find how strange the world becomes in the first mile--and how strange it remains till the common road is reached again.

It always sounds like a mockery for a man who has travelled to a great many places, as I have, to advise his fellows to travel abroad; they are most of them hard tied. Yet it is really a much easier thing than men bound to the desk and the workshop understand. Britain is but one great port, and its inward seas are narrow--and the fares are ridiculously low. If you are a young man you can go almost anywhere for almost anything, sitting up by night on deck, and not expecting too much courtesy. But, of course, if you shirk the sea you are a prisoner.

Well, then, supposing you abroad, or even in some other part of this highly varied kingdom in which you live, and supposing you to have reached some chosen place by some common road--what I

140

desire to dilate upon here is the truth which every little excursion of business or of leisure (and precious few of leisure) makes me more certain of every day: That just a little way off the road is fairyland.

It was exactly three days ago that I had occasion to go down the railway line that is the most frequented in Europe: I was on business, not leisure, but in the business I had two days' leisure, and I did what I would advise all other men to do in such a circumstance.

I took a train to nowhere, fixing my starting-point thus:--

I first looked at the map and saw where nearest to me was a quadrilateral bare of railways. This formula, to look for a quadrilateral bare of railways, is a very useful formula for the man who is seeking another world. Then I fixed at random upon one little roadside station upon the main line; I determined to get out there and to walk aimlessly and westward until I should strike the other side of the quadrilateral. I made no plan, not even of the hours of the day.

I came into my roadside station at half-past eight of the long summer night, broad daylight that is, but with night advancing. I got out and began my westward march. At once there crowded upon me any number of unexpected and entertaining things!

The first thing I found was a street which was used by horses as well as by men, and yet was made up of broad steps. It was a sort of stair-case going up a hill. At the top of it I found a woman leading a child by the hand. I asked her the name of the steps. She told me they were called "The Steps of St. John."

A quarter of a mile further down the narrow lane I saw to my astonishment an enormous castle, ruined and open to the sky. There are many such ruins famous in Europe, but of this one I had never even heard. I went lonely under the evening and looked at its main gate and saw on it a moulded escutcheon, carved, and the motto in French, "Henceforward," which word made me think a great deal, but resolved no problem in my mind.

I went on again westward as the darkness fell and saw what I had not seen before, though my reading had told me of its existence, a long line of trees marking a ridge on the horizon, which line was the border of that ancient road the Roman soldiers built leading from the west into Amiens. "Along that road," thought I, "St. Martin rode before he became a monk, and while he was yet a soldier and was serving under Julian the Apostate. Along that road he came to the west gate of Amiens and there cut his cloak in two and gave the half of it to a beggar."

The memory of St. Martin's deed entertained me for some miles of my way, and I remembered how, when I was a child, it had

141

seemed to me ridiculous to cut your coat in two whether for a beggar or for anybody else. Not that I thought charity ridiculous-- God forbid!--but that a coat seemed to me a thing you could not cut in two with any profit to the user of either half. You might cut it in latitude and turn it into an Eton jacket and a kilt, neither of much use to a Gallo-Roman beggar. Or you might cut it in meridian and leave but one sleeve: mere folly.

Considering these things, I went on over the rolling plateau. I saw a great owl flying before me against the sky, different from the owls of home. I saw Jupiter shining above a cloud and Venus shining below one. The long light lingered in the north above the English sea. At last I came quite unexpectedly upon that delight and plaything of the French: a light railway, or steam tram such as that people build in great profusion to link up their villages and their streams. The road where I came upon it made a level crossing, and there was a hut there, and a woman living in it who kept the level crossing and warned the passers-by. She told me no more trains, or rather little trams, would pass that night, but that three miles further on I should come to a place called "The Mills of the Vidame." Now the name "Vidame" reminded me that a "Vidame" was the lay protector of a Cathedral Chapter in feudal times, so the name gave me a renewed pleasure.

But it was now near midnight, and when I came to this village I remembered how in similar night walks I had sometimes been refused lodging. When I got among the few houses all was dark. I found, however, in the darkness two young men, each bearing an enormous curled trumpet of the kind which the French call cors de chasse, that is, hunting horns, so I asked them where the inn was. They took me to it and woke up the hostess, who received us with oaths. This she did lest the young men with hunting horns should demand a commission. Her heart, however, was better than her mouth, and she put me up, but she charged me tenpence for my room, counting coffee in the morning, which was, I am sure, more than her usual rate.

Next day I took the little steam tram away from the place and went on vaguely whither it should please God to take me, until the plateau changed and the light railway fell into a charming valley, and, seeing a town rooted therein, I got out and paid my fare and visited the town. In this town I went to church, as it was early morning (you must excuse the foible), and, coming out of church, I had an argument with a working man upon the matter of religion, in which argument, as I believe, I was the victor. I then went on north out of this town and came into a wood of enormous size. It was miles and miles across, and the trees were higher than anything I

142

have seen outside of California. It was an enchanted wood. The sun shone down through a hundred feet of silence by little rounds between the leaves, and there was silence everywhere. In this wood I sojourned all day long, making slowly westward, till, in the very midst of it, I found a troubled man. He was a man of middle age, short, intelligent, fat, and weary. He said to me:

"Have you noticed any special mark upon the trees? A white mark of the number 90?"

"No," said I. "Are there any wild boars in this forest?"

"Yes," he answered, "a few, but not of use. I am looking for trees marked in white with the number 90. I have paid a price for them, and I cannot find them."

I saluted him and went on my way. At last I came to an open clearing, where there was a town, and in the town I found a very delightful inn, where they would cook anything one felt inclined for, within reason, and charged one very moderately indeed. I have retained its name.

By this time I was completely lost, and in the heart of Fairyland, when suddenly I remembered that everyone that strikes root in Fairyland loses something, at the least his love and at the worst his soul, and that it is a perilous business to linger there, so I asked them in that hotel how they worked it when they wanted to go west into the great towns. They put me into an omnibus, which charged me fourpence for a journey of some two miles. It took me, as Heaven ordained, to a common great railway, and that common great railway took me through the night to the town of Dieppe, which I have known since I could speak and before, and which was about as much of Fairyland to me as Piccadilly or Monday morning.

Thus ended those two days, in which I had touched again the unknown places--and all that heaven was but two days, and cost me not fifty shillings.

Excuse the folly of this.

The Tide

I wish I had been one of those men who first sailed beyond the Pillars of Hercules and first saw, as they edged northward along a barbarian shore, the slow swinging of the sea. How much, I wonder, did they think themselves enlarged? How much did they know that all the civilization behind them, the very ancient world of the Mediterranean, was something protected and enclosed from which they had escaped into an outer world? And how much did they feel that here they were now physically caught by the moving tides that bore them in the whole movement of things?

For the tide is of that kind; and the movement of the sea four times daily back and forth is a consequence, a reflection, and a part of the ceaseless pulse and rhythm which animates all things made and which links what seems not living to what certainly lives and feels and has power over all movement of its own. The circuits of the planets stretch and then recede. Their ellipses elongate and flatten again to the semblance of circles. The Poles slowly nod once every many thousand years, there is a libration to the moon; and in all this vast harmonious process of come and go the units of it twirl and spin, and, as they spin, run more gravely in ordered procession round their central star: that star moves also to a beat, and all the stars of heaven move each in times of its own as well, and their movement is one thing altogether. Whoever should receive the mighty business moving in one ear would get the music of it in a perfect series of chords, superimposed the one upon the other, but not a tremble of them out of tune.

The great scheme is not infinite, for were it infinite such rhythms could not be. It was made, and it moves in order to the scheme of its making without caprice, not wayward anywhere, but in and out and back and forth as to a figure set for it. It must be so, or these exact arrangements could not be.

Now with this regulated breathing and expiration, playing itself out in a million ways and co-extensive with the universe of things, the tides keep time, and they alone of earthly things bring its actual force to our physical perception, to our daily life. We see the sea in movement and power before us heaving up whatever it may bear, and we feel in an immediate way its strong backward sagging when the rocks appear above it as it falls. We have our hand on the throb of the current turning in a salting river inland between green hills; we are borne upon it bodily as we sail, its movement kicks the tiller in our grasp, and the strength beneath us and around us, the rush and the compulsion of the stream, its silence and as it were its purpose, all represent to us, immediately and here, that immeasurable to and fro which rules the skies.

When the Roman soldiers came marching northward with Caesar and first saw the shores of ocean: when, after that occupation of Gaul which has changed the world, they first mounted guard upon the quays of the Itian port under Gris-Nez, or the rocky inlets of the Veneti by St. Malo and the Breton reefs, they were appalled to see what for centuries chance traders and the few curious travellers, the men of Marseilles and of the islands, had seen before them. They saw in numbers and in a corporate way what hitherto individuals alone had seen; they saw the sea like a living thing, advancing and retreating in an ordered dance, alive with deep sighs and intakes, and ceaselessly proceeding about a work and a doing which seemed to be the very visible action of an unchanging will still pleased with calculated change. It was the presence of the Roman army upon the shores of the Channel which brought the Tide into the general conscience of Europe, and that experience, I think, was among the greatest, perhaps the greatest, of those new things which rushed upon the mind of the Empire when it launched itself by the occupation of Gaul.

The tide, when it is mentioned in brief historical records of times long since, suddenly strikes one with vividness and with familiarity, so that the past is introduced at once, presented to us physically, and obtruded against our modern senses alive. I know of no other physical thing mentioned in this fashion, in chronicle or biography, which has so powerful an effect to restore the reality of a dead century.

The Venerable Bede is speaking in one place of Southampton Water, in his ecclesiastical history, or, rather, of the Isle of Wight, whence those two Princes were baptized and died under Cadwalla. As the historian speaks of the place he says:

"In this sea" (which is the Solent) "comes a double tide out of the seas which spring from the infinite ocean of the Arctic surrounding all Britain."

And he tells us how these double tides rush together and fight together, sweeping as they do round either side of the island by the Needles and by Spithead into the land-locked sheet within.

Now that passage in Bede's fourth book is more real to me than anything in all his chronicle, for in Southampton Water to-day the living thing which we still note as we sail is the double tide. You take a falling tide at the head of the water, near Southampton Town, and if you are not quick with your business it is checked in two hours and you meet a strange flood, the second flood, before you have rounded Calshott Castle.

Then there is a Charter of Newcastle. Or, rather, the inviolable Customs of that town, very old, drawn up nearly eight hundred years ago, but beginning from far earlier; and in these customs you find written:

"If a plea shall arise between a burgess and a merchant it must be determined before the third flowing of the sea"--that is, within three tides; a wise provision! For thus the merchant would not miss the last tide of the day after the quarrel. How living it is, a phrase of that sort coming in the midst of those other phrases!

All the rest, worse luck, has gone. Burgage-tenure, and the economic independence of the humble, and the busy, healthy life of men working to enrich themselves, not others, and that corporate association which was the blood of the Middle Ages, and the power of popular opinion, and, in general, freedom. But out of all these things that have perished, the tide remains, and in the eighteen clauses of the Customs, the tidal clause alone stands fresh and still has meaning. The capital, great clinching clause by which men owned their own land within the town has gone utterly and altogether. The modern workman on the Tyne would not understand you perhaps, to whom in that very place you should say, "Many centuries ago the men that came before you here, your fathers, were not working precariously at a wage, or paying rent to others, but living under their own roofs and working for themselves." There is only one passage in the document that all could understand in Newcastle to-day--the very few rich who are hardly secure, the myriads of poor who are not secure at all--and that passage is the passage which talks of the third tide; for even to-day there is some good we have left undestroyed and the sea still ebbs and flows.

This little note of the Newcastle men, and of the flowing and the ebbing of their sea, is to be found, you say, in the archives of England? Not at all! It is to be found in the Acts of the Parliament of Scotland--at least, so my book assures me, but why I do not know. Perhaps of the times when between Tyne and Tees, men looked northward and of the times when they looked southward (for they alternately did one and the other during many hundreds of years) those times when they looked northward seemed the more natural to them. Anyhow, the reference is to the Acts of the Parliament of Scotland, and that is the end of it.

On a Great Wind

It is an old dispute among men, or rather a dispute as old as mankind, whether Will be a cause of things or no; nor is there anything novel in those moderns who affirm that Will is nothing to the matter, save their ignorant belief that their affirmation is new.

The intelligent process whereby I know that Will not seems but is, and can alone be truly and ultimately a cause, is fed with stuff and strengthens sacramentally as it were, whenever I meet, and am made the companion of, a great wind.

It is not that this lively creature of God is indeed perfected with a soul; this it would be superstition to believe. It has no more a person than any other of its material fellows, but in its vagary of way, in the largeness of its apparent freedom, in its rush of purpose, it seems to mirror the action of mighty spirit. When a great wind comes roaring over the eastern flats towards the North Sea, driving over the Fens and the Wringland, it is like something of this island that must go out and wrestle with the water, or play with it in a game or a battle; and when, upon the western shores, the clouds come bowling up from the horizon, messengers, outriders, or comrades of a gale, it is something of the sea determined to possess the land. The rising and falling of such power, its hesitations, its renewed violence, its fatigue and final repose--all these are symbols of a mind; but more than all the rest, its exultation! It is the shouting and the hurrahing of the wind that suits a man.

Note you, we have not many friends. The older we grow and the better we can sift mankind, the fewer friends we count, although man lives by friendship. But a great wind is every man's friend, and its strength is the strength of good-fellowship; and even doing battle with it is something worthy and well chosen. If there is cruelty in the sea, and terror in high places, and malice lurking in profound darkness, there is no one of these qualities in the wind, but only power. Here is strength too full for such negations as cruelty, as malice, or as fear; and that strength in a solemn manner proves and tests health in our own souls. For with terror (of the sort I mean-- terror of the abyss or panic at remembered pain, and in general, a losing grip of the succours of the mind), and with malice, and with cruelty, and with all the forms of that Evil which lies in wait for men, there is the savour of disease. It is an error to think of such things as power set up in equality against justice and right living. We were not made for them, but rather for influences large and soundly poised; we are not subject to them but to other powers that can always enliven and relieve. It is health in us, I say, to be full of heartiness and of the joy of the world, and of whether we have such health our comfort in a great wind is a good test indeed. No man spends his day upon the mountains when the wind is out, riding against it or pushing forward on foot through the gale, but at the end of his day feels that he has had a great host about him. It is as though he had experienced armies. The days of high winds are days of innumerable sounds, innumerable in variation of tone and of intensity, playing upon and awakening innumerable powers in man. And the days of high wind are days in which a physical compulsion has been about us and we have met pressure and blows, resisted and turned them; it enlivens us with the simulacrum of war by which nations live, and in the just pursuit of which men in companionship are at their noblest.

It is pretended sometimes (less often perhaps now than a dozen years ago) that certain ancient pursuits congenial to man will be lost to him under his new necessities; thus men sometimes talk foolishly of horses being no longer ridden, houses no longer built of wholesome wood and stone, but of metal; meat no more roasted, but only baked; and even of stomachs grown too weak for wine. There is a fashion of saying these things, and much other nastiness. Such talk is (thank God!) mere folly; for man will always at last tend to his end, which is happiness, and he will remember again to do all those things which serve that end. So it is with the uses of the wind, and especially the, using of the wind with sails.

No man has known the wind by any of its names who has not sailed his own boat and felt life in the tiller. Then it is that a man has most to do with the wind, plays with it, coaxes or refuses it, is wary of it all along; yields when he must yield, but comes up and pits himself again against its violence; trains it, harnesses it, calls it if it fails him, denounces it if it will try to be too strong, and in every manner conceivable handles this glorious playmate.

As for those who say that men did but use the wind as an instrument for crossing the sea, and that sails were mere machines to them, either they have never sailed or they were quite unworthy of sailing. It is not an accident that the tall ships of every age of varying fashions so arrested human sight and seemed so splendid. The whole of man went into their creation, and they expressed him very well; his cunning, and his mastery, and his adventurous heart. For the wind is in nothing more capitally our friend than in this, that it has been, since men were men, their ally in the seeking of the unknown and in their divine thirst for travel which, in its several aspects--pilgrimage, conquest, discovery, and, in general,

148

enlargement--is one prime way whereby man fills himself with being.

I love to think of those Norwegian men who set out eagerly before the north-east wind when it came down from their mountains in the month of March like a god of great stature to impel them to the West. They pushed their Long Keels out upon the rollers, grinding the shingle of the beach at the fjord-head. They ran down the calm narrows, they breasted and they met the open sea. Then for days and days they drove under this master of theirs and high friend, having the wind for a sort of captain, and looking always out to the sea line to find what they could find. It was the springtime; and men feel the spring upon the sea even more surely than they feel it upon the land. They were men whose eyes, pale with the foam, watched for a landfall, that unmistakable good sight which the wind brings us to, the cloud that does not change and that comes after the long emptiness of sea days like a vision after the sameness of our common lives. To them the land they so discovered was wholly new.

We have no cause to regret the youth of the world, if indeed the world were ever young. When we imagine in our cities that the wind no longer calls us to such things, it is only our reading that blinds us, and the picture of satiety which our reading breeds is wholly false. Any man to-day may go out and take his pleasure with the wind upon the high seas. He also will make his landfalls to-day, or in a thousand years; and the sight is always the same, and the appetite for such discoveries is wholly satisfied even though he be only sailing, as I have sailed, over seas that he has known from childhood, and come upon an island far away, mapped and well known, and visited for the hundredth time.

The Letter

If you ask me why it is now three weeks since I received your letter and why it is only today that I answer it, I must tell you the truth lest further things I may have to tell you should not be worthy of your dignity or of mine. It was because at first I dared not, then later I reasoned with myself, and so bred delay, and at last took refuge in more delay. I will offer no excuse: I will not tell you that I suffered illness, or that some accident of war had taken me away from this old house, or that I have but just returned from a journey to my hill and my view over the Plain and the great River.

Your messenger I have kept, and I have entertained him well. I looked at him a little narrowly at his first coming, thinking perhaps he might be a gentleman of yours, but I soon found that he was not such, and that he bore no disguise, but was a plain rider of your household. I put him in good quarters by the Hunting Stables. He has had nothing to do but to await my resolution, which is now at last taken, and which you receive in this.

But how shall I begin, or how express to you what not distance but a slow and bitter conclusion of the mind has done?

I shall not return to Meudon. I shall not see the woods, the summer woods turning to autumn, nor follow the hunt, nor take pleasure again in what is still the best of Europe at Versailles. And now that I have said it, you must read it so; for I am unalterably determined. Believe me, it is something much more deep than courtesy which compels me to give you my reasons for this final and irrevocable doom.

We were children together. Though we leant so lightly in our conversations of this spring upon all we knew in common, I know your age and all your strong early experience--and you know mine. Your mother will recall that day's riding when I came back from my first leave and you were home, not, I think, for good, from the convent. A fixed domestic habit blinded her, so that she could then still see in us no more than two children; yet I was proud of my sword, and had it on, and you that day were proud of a beauty which could no longer be hidden even from yourself; I would then have sacrificed, and would now, all I had or was or had or am to have made that beauty immortal.

I say, you remember that day's riding, and how after it the world was changed for you and me, and how that same evening the elders saw that it was changed.

You will remember that for two years we were not allowed to

meet again. When the two years were passed we met indeed by a mere accident of that rich and tedious life wherein we were both now engaged. I was returned from leave before Tournay; you had heard, I think, a false report that I had been wounded in the dreadful business at Fontenoy (which to remember even now horrifies me a little). I had heard and knew which of the great names you now bore by marriage. The next day it was your husband who rode with me to Marly. I liked him well enough. I have grown to like him better. He is an honest man, though I confess his philosophers weary me. When I say "an honest man" I am giving the highest praise I know.

My dear, that was sixteen years ago.

You may not even now understand, so engrossing is the toilsome and excited ritual of that rich world at Versailles, how blest you are: your children are growing round you: your daughters are beginning to reveal your own beauty, and your sons will show in these next years immediately before us that temper which in you was a spirit and a height of being, and in them, men, will show as plain courage. During that long space of years your house has remained well ordered (it was your husband's doing). His great fortune and yours have jointly increased: if I may tell you so, it is a pleasure to all who understand fitness to know that this is so, and that your lineage and his will hold so great a place in the State.

As you review those sixteen years you may, if you will--I trust you will not--recall those occasions when I saw the woods of Meudon and mixed by chance with your world, and when we renewed the rides which had ended our childhood. As for me I have not to recall those things. They are, alas, myself, and beyond them there is nothing that I can call a memory or a being at all. Nevertheless, as I have told you, I shall not come to Meudon: I shall not hear again the delightful voices of those many friends (now in mid-life as am I) who are my equals at Versailles. I shall not see your face.

I did not take service with the Empire from any pique or folly, but from a necessity for adventure and for the refounding of my house. It might have chanced that I should marry: the land demanded an heir. My impoverishment weighed upon me like an ill deed, for all this belt of land is dependent upon the old house, which I can with such difficulty retain and from which I write to-day. I spent all those years in the service of the Empire (and even of Russia) from no uncertain temper and from no imaginary quarrel. It is so common or so necessary for men and women to misjudge each other that I believe you thought me wayward, or at least unstable. If you did so you did me a wrong. Those two good seasons when we met again, and this last of but a month ago, were not accidents or fitful recoveries. They were all I possessed in my life and all that will perish with me when I die.

But now, to tell you the very core of my decision, it is this: The years that pass carry with them an increasing weight at once sombre and majestic. There are things belonging to youth which habit continues strangely longer than the season to which they properly belong: if, when we discover them to be too prolonged as cling to their survival, why, then, we eat dust. So long as we possess the illusion and so long as the dearest things of youth maintain unchanged, in one chamber of our life at least, our twentieth year, so long all is well. But there is a cold river which we must pass in our advance towards nothingness and age. In the passage of that stream we change: and you and I have passed it. There is no more endurance in that young mood of ours than in any other human thing. One always wakes from it at last. One sees what it is. The soul sees and counts with hard eyes the price at which a continuance of such high dreams must be purchased, and the heart has a prevision of the evil that the happy cheat will work as maturity is reached by each of us, and as each of us fully takes on the burden of the world.

Therefore I must not return.

Foolishly and without thinking of real things, acting as though indeed that life of dream and of illusion were still possible to me, I yesterday cut with great care a rose, one from the many that have now grown almost wild upon the great wall overlooking the Danube. Then ... I could not but smile to myself when I remembered how by the time that rose should have reached you every petal would be wasted and fallen in the long week's ride. There is a fixed term of life for roses also as for men. I do not cite this to you by way of parable. I have no heart for tricks of the pen to-night; but the two images came together, and you will understand. If I do not return, it is for the same reason that I could not send the rose.

152

The Regret

Everybody knows, I suppose, that kind of landscape in which hills seem to lie in a regular manner, fold on fold, one range behind the other, until, at last, behind them all some higher and grander range dominates and frames the whole.

The infinite variety of light and air and accident of soil provide all men save those who live in the great plains with examples of this sort. The traveller in the dry air of California or of Spain, watching great distances from the heights, will recollect such landscapes all his life. They were the reward of his long ascents and the visions which attended his effort as he climbed up to the ridge of his horizon. Such a landscape does a man see from the Western edges of the Guadarrama, looking eastward and south toward the very distant hills that guard Toledo and the Gulf of the Tagus. Such a landscape does a man see at sunrise from the highest of the Cevennes looking right eastward to the dawn as it comes up in the pure and cold air beyond the Alps, and shows you the falling of the foothills to the Rhone. And by such a landscape is a man gladdened when upon the escarpments of the Tuolumne he turns back and looks westward over the plain towards the vast range.

The experience of such a sight is one peculiar in travel, or, for that matter, if a man is lucky enough to enjoy it at home, insistent and reiterated upon the mind of the home-dwelling man. Such a landscape, for instance, makes a man praise God if his house is upon the height of Mendip, and he can look over falling hills right over the Vale of Severn toward the ridge above ridge of the Welsh solemnities beyond, until the straight line and high of the Black Mountains ends his view.

It is the character of these landscapes to suggest at once a vastness, diversity, and seclusion. When a man comes upon them unexpectedly he can forget the perpetual toil of men and imagine that those who dwell below in the near side before him are exempt from the necessities of this world. When such a landscape is part of a man's dwelling-place, though he well knows that the painful life of men within those hills is the same hard business that it is throughout the world, yet his knowledge is modified and comforted by the permanent glory of the thing he sees.

The distant and high range that bounds his view makes a sort of veiling, cutting it off and guarding it from whatever may be beyond. The succession of lower ranges suggests secluded valleys, and the reiterated woods, distant and more distant, convey an impression of fertility more powerful than that of corn in harvest upon the lowlands.

Sometimes it is a whole province that is thus grasped by the eye, sometimes in the summer haze but a few miles; always this scenery inspires the onlooker with a sense of completion and of repose, and at the same time, I think, with worship and with awe.

Now one such group of valleys there was, hill above hill, forest above forest, and beyond it a great noble range, unwooded and high against heaven, guarding it, which I for my part knew when first I knew anything of this world. There is a high place under fir trees, a place of sand and bracken, in South England whence such a view was always present to eye in childhood and "There," said I to myself (even in childhood) "a man should make his habitation." In those valleys is the proper off-set for man.

And so there was.

It was a little place which had grown up as my county grows. The house throwing out arms and layers. One room was panelled in the oak of the seventeenth century--but that had been a novelty in its time, for the walls upon which the panels stood were of the late fifteenth, oak and brick intermingled. Another room was large and light built in the manner of one hundred and fifty years ago, which people call Georgian. It had been thrown out south (which is quite against our older custom, for our older houses looked east and west to take all the sun and to present a corner to the south-west and the storms. So they stand still). It had round it a solid cornice which the modern men of the towns would have called ugly, but there was ancestry in it. Then, further on this house had modern roominess stretching in one new wing after another; and it had a great steading and there was a copse and some six acres of land. Over a deep ravine looked the little town that was the mother of the place, and altogether it was enclosed, silent, and secure.

"The fish that misses the hook regrets the worm." If this is not a Chinese proverb it ought to be. That little farm and steading and those six acres, that ravine, those trees, that aspect of the little mothering town; the wooded hills fold above fold, the noble range beyond, will not be mine.

For all I know, some man quite unacquainted with that land took them grumbling for a debt; or again, for all I know, they may have been bought by a blind man who could not see the hills, or by some man who, seeing them, perpetually regretted the flat marshes of the fens. One day, up high on Egdean Side, not thinking of such things, through a gap in the trees I saw again after so many years, set one behind the other, the forests wave upon wave, the summer

154

heat, the high, bare range guarding all, and in the midst of that landscape, set like a toy, the little Sabine Farm.

Then I said to it, "Continue. Go and serve whom you will, my little Sabine Farm. You were not mine because you would not be, and you are not mine at all to-day. You will regret it perhaps, and perhaps you will not. There was verse in you, perhaps, or prose, or--infinitely more!--contentment for a man (for all I know). But you refused. You lost your chance. Goodbye." And with that I went on into the wood and beyond the gap, and saw the sight no more.

It was ten years since I had seen it last. It may be ten years before I see it again, or it may be for ever. But as I went through the woods saying to myself:

"You lost your chance, my little Sabine Farm, you lost your chance!" another part of me at once replied:

"Ah! And so did you!"

Then, by way of riposte, I answered in my mind:

"Not at all, for the chance I never had, but what I lost was my desire."

"No, not your desire," said the voice to me within, "but the fulfilment of it, in which you would have lost your desire." And when that reply came I naturally turned as all men do on hearing such interior replies, to a general consideration of regret, and was prepared, if any honest publisher should have come whistling through that wood, with an offer proper to the occasion, namely, to produce no less than five volumes on the Nature of Regret, its mortal sting, its bitter-sweetness, its power to keep alive in man the pure passions of the soul, its hints at immortality, its memory of Heaven. But the wood was empty of publishers. The offer did not come. The moment was lost. The five volumes will hardly now be written. In place of them I offer poor this, which you may take or leave. But I beg leave before I end to cite certain words very nobly attached to that great inn "The Griffin," which has its foundation set far off in another place, in the town of March, in the Fen Land:

"England my desire, what have you not refused?"

155

The End Of The World

One day I met a man who was sitting quite silent near Whitney, in the Thames Valley, in a very large, long, low inn that stands in those parts, or at least stood then, for whether it stands now or not depends upon the Fussyites, whose business it is to Fuss, and in their Fussing to disturb mankind.

He had nothing to say for himself at all, and he looked not gloomy but sad. He was tall and thin, with high cheekbones. His face was the colour of leather that has been some time in the weather, and he despised us altogether: he would not say a word to us, until one of the company said, rising from his meat and drink: "Very well, there's a thing we shall never know till the end of the world" (he was talking about some discussion or other which the young men had been holding together). "There's a thing we shall never know till the end of the world--and about that nobody knows!"

"You will pardon me," said the tall, thin, and elderly man with a face like leather that has been exposed to the weather, "I know about the End of the World, for I have been there."

This was so interesting that we all sat down again to listen.

"I wasn't talking of place, but of time," murmured the young man whom the stranger had answered.

"I cannot help that," said the stranger decisively; "the End of the World is the End of the World, and whether you are talking of space or of time it does not matter, for when you have got to the end you have got to the end, as may be proved in several ways."

"How did you get to it?" said one of our companions.

"That is very simply answered," said the elder man; "you get to it by walking straight in front of you."

"Anyone could do that," said the other.

"Anyone could," said the elder man, "but nobody does. I did.... When I was quite a boy in my father's parsonage (for my father was a parson), having heard so much about the End of the World and seeing that people's descriptions of it differed so much and that everybody was quite sure of his own, I used to take my father's friends and guests aside privately, for I was afraid to take my father himself, and I used to ask them how they knew what the End of the World was really like, and whether they had seen it. Some laughed, others were silent, and others were angry; but no one gave me any information. At last I decided (and it was very wise of me) that the only way to find out a thing of that sort was to find it out for one's

156

self, and not to go by hearsay, so I determined to go straight on without stopping until I got to the End of the World."

"Which way did you walk?" said yet another of my companions.

"Young man," said the stranger, with solemnity, "I walked westward toward the setting sun ... I walked and I walked and I walked, day after day and year after year. Whenever I came to the seacoast I would take work on board a ship--and remember it is always easy to get work if you will take the wages that are offered, and always difficult to get it if you will not. Well, then, I went in this way through all known lands and over all known seas, until at last I came to the shore of a sea beyond which (so the people told me who lived there) there was no further shore. 'I cannot help that,' said I; 'I have not yet come to the End of the World, and it is common sense that such a lot of water must have something at the back of it to hold it up; besides which there is a strong wind blowing out of the gates of the west and from the sunset. Now that wind must rise somewhere, and I am going on to see where it rises.' One of them was kind enough to lend me a boat with oars; I thanked him prettily, and then I set out to row toward the End of the World, taking with me two or three days' provisions.

"When I had rowed a long time I went asleep, and when I woke up next morning I rowed again all day until the second night I went to sleep. On the third day I rowed again: a little before sunset on the third day I saw before me high hills, all in peaks like a great saw. On the very highest of the peaks there were streaks of snow, and at about six o'clock in the afternoon I grounded my boat upon that gravelly shore and pulled it up upon the shingle, though it was evident either that the tide was high or that there was no tide in these silent places.

"I offered up a prayer to the genius of the land, and tied the painter of the boat to two great stones, so that no wave reaching it might move it, and then I went on inland. When I had gone a little way I saw a signpost on which was written, 'To the End of the World One Mile' and there was a rough track along which it pointed. I went along this track. Everything was completely silent. There were no birds, there was no wind, there was nothing in the sky. But one thing I did notice, which was that the sun was much larger than it used to be, and that as I went along this last mile or so it seemed to get larger still--but that may have been my imagination, for I must tell you my imagination is pretty strong.

"Well then, gentlemen, when I had gone a mile or so I saw another signpost, on which there was a large board marked 'Danger,' and a hundred yards beyond the track went between two great dark rocks--and there I was! The road had stopped short; it was broken off, jagged, just like a torn bit of paper ... and there was the End of the World."

"How do you mean?" said one of the younger men in an awed tone.

"What I say," said the stranger decidedly. "I had come to the end; there was nothing beyond. You looked down over a precipice where there was moss and steep grass, and on the ledges trees far below, and then more precipice, and then--oh, miles below--a few more trees or so clinging to the steep, then more precipice, and then darkness; and far away before me was the whole expanse of sky; and in the midst of it I saw the broad red sun setting into the brume; it was not yet dark enough to see the stars, and there was no moon in the sky.

"I assure you it was a very wonderful sight, and I was awed though I was not afraid. And how glad I was to find that the world had an edge to it, and that all that talk about its being round was nonsense!

"When the sun was set it grew dark, and I returned to find my boat; but I must have missed my way, for the track became broader and better, and at last I came to a gate of a human sort, with an initial on it, which showed that it had been put up by some landlord. It was an open gate, and after I had entered it I came upon a broad highway, beautifully metalled, and when I had gone along this for less than half a mile I came to this inn where I am now sitting. That was a week ago, and I have been here ever since. They took me in kindly enough, but they would not believe what I had to tell them about the End of the World. It is a great pity, gentlemen, for that wonderful sight is to be discovered somewhere hereabouts, and a mere accident of my losing my way in the darkness makes it difficult for me to find it by daylight."

Having said all this, the stranger was silent.

One of my companions whispered to me that the old man must be mad. The stranger overheard him, and said with a thin smile:

"Oh, I know all about that; several have suggested it already; but it is no answer, for if I did not come from the End of the World, where did I come from? No one has seen me hereabouts during the last few days until I came to this inn. And all the first part of my journey I can very easily explain, for I have notes of it, and it lasted for years. It is only this last part which seems to me so difficult.... I tell you I lost my way, and when a man has lost his way at night he can never find it again in the daytime."

As he spoke he took a little piece of folded paper, rather dirty, out of his inner pocket, on which a rough sketch-map was drawn, and he began touching it with a stump of pencil that he held in his hand. His eyes seemed to grow dimmer as he did so, and he leaned his head upon his hand. "I think I have got hold of it, gentlemen," he said.

We did not get up or go too near him, for we thought he might be dangerous.

"I think, gentlemen," he repeated in a more mumbling and lower and less certain voice, "I think I have got hold of it. I go backwards again through the gate to the right, just as then I went to the left, and after that it cannot be very far, for I see those two rocks in front of me. Besides which," he muttered less and less coherently, "I ought to have remembered of course those very high and silent hills with nothing living upon them...." And he added, half asleep, as his head dropped upon his hand, "It was westward.... I had forgotten that." Having so spoken, he seemed to fall asleep altogether, and his head fell back upon the corner of the wainscoting behind the bench where he sat. He made no noise in breathing as he slept.

It was the first time that any of us young men had come across this fairly common sight of a man who took things within for things without; some of us were frightened, and all of us wished to be rid of the place and to get away. As we went out we told the landlord nothing either of the old fellow's vagaries or of his sleep, but we went out and reached the town of Whitney, and when we had stayed there a couple of hours or so we went out southward to the station and waited there for the train which should take us back to Oxford.

While we were waiting there in the station two farmers were talking together. One said to the other:

"Ar, if he'd paid them they wouldn't have minded so much."

To which the other answered:

"Ar, 'tisn't only the paying: it's always an awkward thing when a man dies in your house, specially if it's licensed. My wife's brother was caught that way."

Then as they went on talking we found that they were talking of the man in the inn, who it seems had not slept very long, but was dead, and had died in that same room. It was a shocking thing to hear. The first farmer said to the second in the railway carriage when we had all got in:

"Where'd he come from?"

The other, who was an old man, grinned and said:

"Where we all come from, I suppose, and where we all go to." He touched his forehead with his hand. "He said he'd come from the End of the World."

"Ar," said the other gloomily in answer, "like enough!" And after that they talked no more about the matter.